FINDING JENNIFER JONES

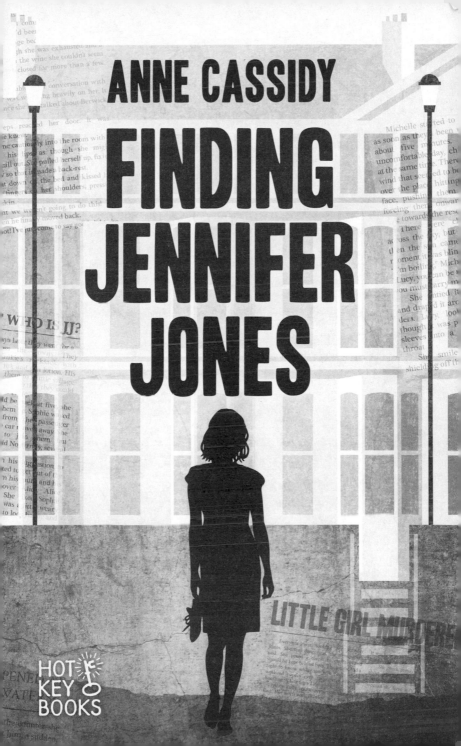

ANNE CASSIDY

FINDING JENNIFER JONES

HOT KEY BOOKS

First published in Great Britain in 2014 by Hot Key Books
Northburgh House, 10 Northburgh Street, London EC1V 0AT

A CIP catalogue record for this book is available from the British Library.

ISBN: 978-1-4714-0228-9

1

This book is typeset in 10.5 Berling LT Std using Atomik ePublisher

Printed and bound by Clays Ltd, St Ives Plc

FSC

Hot Key Books supports the Forest Stewardship Council (FSC),
the leading international forest certification organisation, and is
committed to printing only on Greenpeace-approved FSC-certified paper.

www.hotkeybooks.com

Hot Key Books is part of the Bonnier Publishing Group
www.bonnierpublishing.com

For Terry with much love

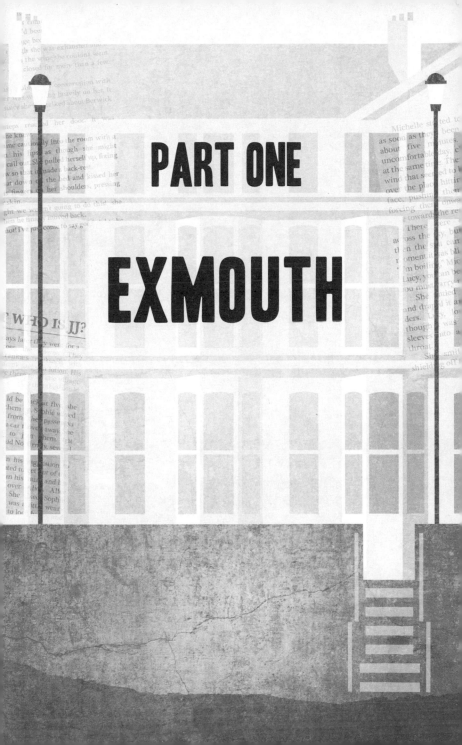

PART ONE

EXMOUTH

ONE

Kate Rickman looked down at her hands.

Hands that had killed.

She held them flat, palms down. Her hands were pale, a threadwork of veins just visible underneath the skin. The fingers were thin and seemed to tremble as she stared at them. The nails were short. There was no varnish and no rings; no decoration of any kind.

She was standing on the esplanade leaning on the wall. Below her there were families on the beach. They had camped in little groups with wind breakers curved protectively around them. In front of her the sea was restless, shrugging wave after wave towards the shore. Small children were standing in frilly costumes looking down with delight at the frothing water.

Kate heard her ringtone and pulled her phone out of her pocket.

It was a message from Aimee at work.

Kate will you come into work an hour early tomorrow?
Be so grateful ☺

Kate looked back to the beach. There was a young woman with a small girl, about three years old. She had her arms held out as if she wanted to be cuddled. The woman was not much older than Kate herself. She was wearing cut-offs and a vest. She was talking into a mobile phone, gesticulating with her free hand. The toddler began to cry and the woman glanced down and grabbed her by one arm and pulled her back up the beach. All the time she continued her conversation on her phone.

Kate turned away from the water, her elbows on the wall. Her hair blew back, some single strands sticking to her face. She licked her lips and tasted the saltiness of the sea.

She thought of the letter she had posted a few days before.

She pictured a sixteen-year-old girl frowning as she read the handwritten pages. Nowadays it was all emails and texts. Why would someone go to the trouble of writing line after line? Had she even read it? Or had she thrown it away as soon as she saw the signature at the bottom?

Jennifer Jones

The sound of a police siren cut through the air. It startled Kate and her eye followed the car as it shunted along the esplanade trying to get past queuing traffic. It swung round the side of an ice-cream van and sped off towards the far end of the resort. Another car followed it rapidly although it had no blue flashing lights.

Then it was quiet, just the splash of the sea and voices calling out. From below, on the beach, was the scratchy sound of someone's radio.

Her mobile beeped again. On the screen she could see the message icon. It was from her probation officer. Sighing, she opened it.

Don't forget your appt this week. Friday 5.30pm

She put the mobile back in her pocket, a feeling of irritation niggling at her. She lifted her face up to the sun, closing her eyes tightly. How many more *appointments* would there be for her? Doctors? Counsellors? Probation officers? Would they ever, finally, let her go?

In the distance, many streets away, a car horn sounded. Kate turned away from it and faced the sea. The water was glittering as if there were jewels floating on its surface. She wished she was out there, immersed in it, only the sound of the surf in her ears.

Instead she was marooned on the shore. She looked at her hands again. Now they were in fists, curled up tight like rosebuds.

A long time ago they had taken the life of a child.

There would never be any freedom for her.

TWO

"So, Kate, how have you been?" Julia said.

"Good."

"You missed the last session. I was concerned."

"I did ring and leave a message."

"That's not quite the point."

Julia Masters stared at her. Kate looked away. They were in Julia's office and as usual it was neat and tidy, like a showroom. The desk was uncluttered, with just a computer screen and tiny laptop visible. The photos of her family sat alongside the screen, two boys; Justin and Peter, seven and eight. *Peter is a smashing chess player*, Julia had said, *but Justin is a total bookworm*. On top of Julia's filing cabinet was a tray holding a number of files. One of them, Kate was sure, had her name on it.

"These sessions are mandatory, Kate."

"I'm sorry," she said.

They were not sitting at Julia's desk but in an area of the room that was laid out with armchairs. Julia was sitting in a new chair, Kate noticed. The old one, with its frayed arms and scuffed legs, had been replaced. Kate had spent many hours looking at parts of that armchair, trying to avoid too much eye contact with Julia, her mentor, part of the probation team who looked after her. *We would like you to think of us as friends,* Julia had said, when Kate first met her a year ago. Her previous probation officer had found a new job in a different part of the country and Kate had been passed on. Julia was her third probation officer.

"Just because it's two and a half years since your release it doesn't mean you can afford to be casual about things. Your visits here are as important as they ever were."

"I know," Kate said. How could she not know with all the reminders that Julia sent?

"So, perhaps we should talk about things in general."

Kate tried to concentrate on Julia's face but after a few seconds her eyes began to wander the room. On the walls were framed photographs of the coast; the groynes on the beach, a boat sitting amid the shingle, a gull perched on a rock. The photos were in black and white and gave the impression of overcast dull days.

"Have you anything you'd like to say?" Julia said, brusquely.

Kate looked back to Julia. She was wearing her black jet earrings. They hung low and swung when she moved her head. Her hair had just been washed, Kate thought, it had that bouncy quality that she noticed from time to time.

"About what? Specifically?"

Kate wished Julia could get to the point. Her questions were like nets. She threw them widely.

"I'm concerned that in the past few months – well, six months or so – things haven't been quite so good with you. What's your view?"

"I'm not sure what you mean."

But Kate did know what she meant. Julia was intent on listing her recent failings. Kate wasn't troubled by this. She had done far worse in the past.

"Well." Julia pulled a pad from her bag. "Let me see, I've made some notes."

Kate watched her flick through the pages of a notebook.

"As I said, you've missed a couple of appointments and you missed a random drug test a month or so ago."

"I lost my phone. It was two days before I found it in a friend's house. That's why I didn't come to the drugs test."

"The idea, Kate, as you well know, is that a drugs test is a call that had to be answered and responded to within six hours."

"I lost my phone."

"It won't surprise you if I tell you that it's not the first time I have heard that excuse."

"I came as soon as I found it."

Kate was irked. She'd been telling the truth. She had left her phone in the bedroom of a boy she had met. It was a couple of days before she got it back.

"And the drugs test was clear."

"I don't do drugs. I've told you that," she said, crossing her arms.

Julia frowned. She looked as though she was about to write something down but changed her mind.

"You've turned up for at least two meetings smelling of alcohol. As those meetings were in the morning I'm surmising that the alcohol was consumed the night before?"

"It's just a few glasses of wine. It's not illegal."

"Then there is the time you missed on your course. Your attendance has been very poor this year. Your mentor said he hardly saw you in the summer term."

"I got my work in."

Lately, getting her essays in on time had been a last-minute sprint. Flipping open her laptop, reading her work over rapidly as though it was a shopping list. Then she pressed the *send* button minutes before the university deadline. Once or twice she'd hesitated and thought, *Why bother? What does it matter?*

"Your work was a very low standard. In comparison to previous grades."

"The course is harder than I thought."

Kate pulled a tissue out of her pocket and toyed with it, tearing a strip off from the side. The work wasn't *hard*. She liked the seminars and the tutorials. She enjoyed reading about the distant past, making sense of what happened there. But when it came to getting marks for it or graded she baulked.

"I don't believe you. I think you've given up."

Kate shrugged. What was the point in her trying to explain? Getting a first class degree wouldn't change any of the things that really mattered.

Julia shuffled her papers.

"And the summer job?"

"I like it."

"But at some point you need to start thinking about what you will do next year when you've finished your degree. What career you will decide on."

"I can't think that far ahead. I do know I want to stay in Exmouth. As long as I can get a job that pays my rent I'll be happy."

15

Kate knew that her answer would disappoint Julia. When Julia first became her probation officer she'd talked about Kate doing a Masters or possibly working as an intern for a large company. She'd even suggested that Kate might think of museum work; a curator or researcher.

"How are you settling on the antidepressants?" Julia said, changing the subject.

"I think they're helping."

Kate thought of the prescription that she had picked up a day or two ago from the pharmacy. Just a slim cardboard box holding two foil sheets of pills. It seemed an odd remedy to the thoughts and emotions that had plagued her. Day after day she used her thumb to pop the pill out of a plastic bubble and then swallow it. It was so small she didn't even need a gulp of water to make it go down.

"You've been on them for what? Nine months?"

It was Julia who had raised the possibility of her taking the pills. At first she had been outraged. *I'm not mad!* she'd said. But Julia had gone on to explain how they might help her manage from day to day. *Lots of people take them!* she'd said. *Probation officers?* Kate had asked.

"I don't feel so anxious all the time. At least I seem to have stopped looking over my shoulder every minute of the day."

"That's good. You do have to move on from that period your life. It was eight years ago. You're a different person now."

Kate sighed. "That's not quite true, is it?"

"What do you mean?"

"I took someone's life away. I'm still that person. Nothing can change what I did."

16

An image of Michelle Livingstone's red hair flashed in Kate's mind. She pushed it away.

Julia looked uncomfortable. She preferred to skirt around things. A real conversation where things were said always seemed to make her edgy. Any moment now she would mention the time or targets or tell Kate some little bit of gossip just so that they didn't have to float out into the dangerous waters of what Kate actually did eight years before.

"What I'd like us to agree on…" Julia started.

Kate closed her eyes. It was time for plans.

"I'm sorry, Kate, am I irritating you?"

"No, I'm just not in the mood for this kind of discussion."

"Well, you do not have a choice in this matter. Your continuing freedom demands that you accept certain parameters…"

"What freedom? I can't go anywhere without you knowing. I'm not even allowed to have a passport."

"Goodness! You are not *incarcerated*. You are living among law-abiding people. You are a student, you come and go as you please. How much more freedom can you have?"

Julia was clearly exasperated. She closed her pad, resting her hands on it as if to shut away all the troublesome notes she had written.

"What if I went back to prison?"

"What an extraordinary thing to say."

Julia's mouth was open and she glared straight at Kate without seeming to blink. Then she shook her head slowly. Kate suddenly felt flustered and averted her eyes. She looked at the pictures on the wall, feeling the weight of Julia's stare.

"I mean… Well, it could happen…"

It was something she'd thought of for a while. She couldn't deny it. Going back to prison where she was a true inmate, where she wasn't pretending to be another person. Kate folded her arms. She would never make Julia understand.

"I think it's my job to make sure that doesn't happen," Julia said, standing up, brushing her clothes down as though she had somewhere she had to rush off to. "That said, I think we've probably covered enough ground today. We should meet again next week to make up for the missed session. Say Friday again, five thirty."

Kate stared at the new chair. It was smooth and shiny. A replacement for the old one. Just like Julia was a replacement for a previous probation officer.

"And I would just warn you to be careful of saying things about going back to prison. You were in a children's institution. I can assure you that adult women's facilities are a much more unpleasant experience."

Kate didn't answer, just grabbed her bag and stood up.

"Next Friday at five thirty," Julia called out as Kate left the office.

She went straight home after the meeting. The house was empty and she found herself restless, pacing around, starting to make something to eat and then stopping. She was always like this after a meeting with Julia. She thought about having a shower, getting changed, the evening ahead. Sally, her housemate, had suggested they spend the evening in together. Ruth, the other girl who lived there, would be in soon and most probably bring her boyfriend Robbie home with her. They could get a takeaway. They often did on Fridays.

But Kate couldn't imagine herself doing either of those things.

She looked out of the window. The sun was still strong. There were hours of daylight left. She got undressed, opened her drawer, took out her swimming costume and put it on. She pulled on jeans and a top and put her sandals on. She picked up her towel, her straw beach mat and a book. She went downstairs and packed some bread, cheese and fruit. Also a screw-top bottle of wine and a plastic glass.

She needed a swim and some time on the beach. Maybe then she would feel less tense.

She jumped on the bus heading for Sandy Bay, an area at the eastern end of Exmouth beach. The main beach at Exmouth had a gentle curve and flat yellow sand. Sandy Bay had sharp edges and rocky inlets and she liked it better there. She got off the bus and headed for the coastal path which started to take her upland and past the caravan and mobile home parks. She passed by families who had packed up for the day and were heading back to where they were staying.

The beach was not too busy. There were a few families left and some young teenage boys playing a kind of makeshift handball. She found a place to sit and unrolled her straw mat and unpacked her towel. Then she slipped off her jeans and top and headed for the water. She ran a few steps, the shingle biting at her feet, and then took a dive, plunging in.

She hardly had time to gasp because the momentum carried her swiftly deep underwater where it was black and there was no sound, as if both ears were stuffed with cotton wool. She surfaced moments later, shaking her head, her wet hair streaking her face. She trod water and found herself rising and falling. There were no waves but the sea was undulating, seesawing.

She swam out, twenty, forty, fifty strokes. Now the beach looked small and she felt like she was in the middle of an ocean. She lay on her back and looked up at the sky. There were vapour trails across it and the sun was low. She closed her eyes and felt the water holding her up. She could do anything here and no one could stop her. She swam out further, feeling the water temperature lower. Glancing down she fancied she could see the depth increasing, miles and miles of life and vegetation beneath her. She felt precarious, like she was hanging over the top of the unknown.

She flipped over and headed back towards the beach, her strokes taking armfuls of water and flinging it behind her. In moments she was touching the bottom, her toes feeling the thick wetness of the shore.

She dried herself and sat on her straw mat looking out to sea.

It was gone seven o'clock but still warm enough to sit there in her wet costume so she started her picnic and drank some wine. Across the beach some girls were playing. They were wearing their swimsuits with T-shirts over them. They were lined up and singing like a girl band, one of them pretending to hold a microphone. When they finished their song they laughed and elbowed each other.

The sight of them made Kate smile.

It made her think again of the letter she had sent. So far there had been no reply. Had she expected one? She'd taken a chance sending it at all. Every part of her knew that. It was part of the conditions of her release that she should never contact any of the people involved in that terrible day eight years ago. Julia had reiterated this from time to time. *Under no circumstances must you make any contact either physically or by any other means with a person or persons involved in the events at Berwick Waters.*

Kate thought of the names of those involved.

Lucy Bussell; Michelle's parents – Donna and Frank Livingstone.

But Kate had had things she needed to say so she had written *Dear Lucy* and signed it *Yours, Jennifer Jones.*

She started to pack up her stuff. She decided to walk further up the coastal path and find a place on the top of the cliffs to sit and watch the sun go down. She had her book and the rest of the wine and some fruit.

She'd have a solitary picnic.

She spent a lot of time alone; it suited her.

THREE

On Saturday, at just after ten, Kate walked into the tourist information office for her shift. Aimee was talking to an elderly couple, pointing at a map she had unfolded. She stopped for a minute and smiled. Kate headed behind the counter.

"Oh, Kate," Aimee said, breaking off from her explanation, "Those arrived early this morning. It's the fliers for the attractions. Could you take them into the storeroom and unpack them?"

"Sure."

Kate saw two small brown cardboard boxes one on top of the other by the door. She picked them up and carried them round the counter into the small staff kitchen and put them down on the table. She opened her locker and took out the hanger which held her work blouse. It was pale blue and had the words *Exmouth Tourist Information* imprinted on the fabric. She peeled off her T-shirt and put it on. She buttoned it up and then wriggled around a bit, pulling it straight. Even though it was her size it didn't quite fit and she never felt very comfortable in it. She looked for the new child-friendly badge that Aimee insisted they all wore. It wasn't in her locker. She tutted and plucked up one of the others that were there and pinned it on.

A bell sounded from the shop. Kate headed out in case more holidaymakers had come in and were waiting. It was just the elderly couple leaving though. Aimee was folding up a map she had been using to show them places to go.

"Would it kill those people to pay a pound for a map? Would it? Why come on holiday to a place if you don't want to explore it? Mind you, why come on holiday here at all? When you could go to Spain. Beats me!"

"Then we'd be out of a job," Kate said. 'Has it been busy?'

"So, so. But we have a number of coach parties visiting later today and I was hoping you would display those fliers," Aimee said, pointing to a wall of brown wood pockets which held wads of leaflets for local attractions.

"Sure."

Kate went into the staff area and picked up handfuls of leaflets. She took them back into the shop and began to sort through them.

"You heard about the drowning?" Aimee said.

"No. When? Where? What happened?"

"Last night. It was on the local news website this morning and I heard some people talking about it in the paper shop. Some teenagers going swimming at Sandy Bay. That's all I know."

"I was over at Sandy Bay last night. I didn't see any sign of trouble."

She was frowning though. The tides could be dangerous and the sea bed dropped away quickly in places. She loved swimming in the sea but she knew she had to treat it with respect.

23

"It's not good for the town," Aimee added.

Kate nodded. In June a man had fallen from the Starcross ferry. It was a terrible thing to happen and it upset everyone for ages. The people who worked in the town seemed to take it personally, as though it was one of their own family who had died. It happened the Saturday before she started work at the tourist information office.

She began to file the leaflets into the wooden pockets. She did it automatically, without concentrating, musing on what she had just heard.

The man's body had washed up near Starcross days later. It gave her a bad feeling to think about it. She remembered how people had said he'd had a suit, shirt and tie on, as though he was dressed smartly to go out somewhere. She exhaled. Now someone else had drowned, but they didn't know who or how. She ruffled her fingers through her hair and felt some knots in it. She pulled at them. She knew she had to shake these thoughts from her mind. Every counsellor she'd ever seen had told her not to dwell on morbid subjects. She had enough of her own dark places to keep clear of.

"Do you want a coffee?" she asked.

"Sure. And see if there are any of those chocolate digestives left."

"I thought you were on a diet?" Kate said, smiling, trying to make a joke.

"Just a couple. See me through to lunch. That reminds me. Two weeks today is your last day at work so we'll have to get a cake of some sort. Maybe I'll bake it!"

Kate brought the drinks and biscuits out to Aimee in the shop and then spent some time on the computer identifying accommodation vacancies and looking through emails and enquiries. Aimee preferred it if Kate did this work. She liked to talk to customers and hated working on the computer. Kate didn't mind. This was the latest in a long line of jobs she had done since coming to Exeter University. She'd been a waitress, a postal worker, a shelf stacker and a cleaner. She liked working. It meant that holiday time was filled up and it gave her some money in the bank. When she finished updating the computer she made some phone calls and looked at the rotas for the following week.

Later a couple of police cars went by, their sirens on. Kate frowned and went on to the local news website. Her face fell when she saw the headline. It had been updated an hour before.

Child Feared Drowned at Sandy Bay
A nine-year-old girl is missing in the Sandy Bay area. The incident happened between nine and midnight on Friday evening. Her teenage brother and friends were partying on the beach and the child joined them. Witnesses say that she went into the water by herself. The alarm was not raised until after midnight when the girl was missed. Holidaymakers have been helping in the search. The police have an open mind about this case and say they are not yet looking for a body. "There is every chance that this little girl will be found alive," a police spokesperson said.

Kate logged off, the story giving her a shiver. A *child* had died. It made it ten times worse. The loss of a child with a lifetime ahead of her. Kate found herself staring at the computer screen with her hands clasped tightly. She knew what that meant only too well.

Later on, when it was quiet, Aimee talked about her daughter, Louise. She'd had her sixth birthday party the previous Sunday.

"Her dad said he'd come. He promised her faithfully he'd come with a huge surprise. Well, the surprise was he didn't show up. No surprise to me, of course, but Louise was so upset and tearful. It's not fair. Do you think it's fair? It's not fair."

Aimee wasn't really expecting an answer so Kate didn't give one.

"And then he rings me this morning and says he wants to take her away this weekend to make up for it. He's going to take her to Croyde. Well, I know what that means. He's got a surfing weekend with his mates and he will take Louise and dump her with a load of other surfers' kids while he goes off enjoying himself. That's not right. Is it? Do you think that's right?"

There was silence and Kate realised that this time Aimee did expect an answer.

"Not if that's what he does," Kate said. What was she supposed to say?

"Last time he took her – Easter I think it was – she told me she woke up in the middle of the night and there was a lady standing in the hallway with just her knickers on! See, he doesn't mind his daughter witnessing his goings-on!"

The door opened and some people came into the shop. Aimee broke into a big smile and began to talk to them. Kate spent some time helping a young couple find accommodation in a youth hostel. Outside she noticed another police car passing. It didn't have its siren on but still it looked ominous.

Kate spent the rest of her shift making theatre reservations for holidaymakers who had booked through their hotels to see shows in Exeter and Newton Abbot. She sent out the daily newsletter highlighting the events that would happen in the next couple of days, Sunday and Monday. Aimee left just after three thirty and it was up to her to sort out the office and get ready for Monday, then lock up at four.

The house was quiet when she got home. She went straight upstairs to her room and pulled her clothes off. She was hot and sticky so she had a shower. Afterwards she sat in her room with the towel tied around her. The evening lay ahead of her. Tomorrow was Sunday so no work, no need to get up early. She looked around her room. There was washing and ironing she could do. She could watch a movie with Ruth and Robbie. Or see what Sally was doing. Or she could listen to some music in her room.

She stood up and looked out of the bay window towards the sea. The house was in a backstreet, but because of the incline and the fact that it was on the end of a terrace Kate had a partial sea view. She stared at the surface which looked blue and calm, a flat sheet of water.

Someone had drowned in it, though.

Kate flipped open her laptop and glanced over the reports. The child's body had not washed up but the girl had been named, *Jodie Mills*. Nine years old.

Eight years before she had seen Lucy Bussell almost drown in the lake at Berwick Waters. Kate had saved her life that day, but that was only fair because it was she who had pushed her into the water in the first place. The memory made her restless, unhappy. She got up and paced up and down her room. The whole day had been like this. Ever since she'd heard about the drowning her mind had been pulled back to the past and it was not a place where she liked to dwell. Then she had been Jennifer Jones. Then she had stood looking down at the body of her best friend. In her head she tried to close it off and focus on something else, but the only other thing she could think of was the girl in the water at Sandy Bay

Her body would wash up onto one of the beaches. Then the police sirens would sing out mournfully along the esplanade and the people in the town would speak in quiet tones and look towards Sandy Bay with sorrow. How long would it take? Would it be tonight? Tomorrow? Or days later, like the man who fell off the ferry?

It was making Kate feel fearful. She couldn't stay in.

She rummaged about in her wardrobe for a clean skirt and top. She brushed her hair roughly, but it was too tangled and the bristles kept catching on knotted bits. She flung the brush down, picked up her bag and her phone and went out of her room.

The front door opened as she went downstairs. It was Sally, holding a bag of shopping in one hand.

"Hi," she said, "I was going to cook…"

"Not for me, Sal, thanks," Kate said.

"Where are you going?"

Kate didn't know. She just had to get out.

"Not sure. Might meet up with some friends. See you later."

The door closed behind her. She felt lighter immediately. The smell of the sea was strong and she headed towards it.

FOUR

Kate woke up the next morning. The room was in semi darkness. A single shaft of light split the gloom. She let her eyes travel along it. It took her a few moments to realise that her mouth was dry and her head felt heavy. The clock showed that it was 09:51. She pulled the pillow to the side to get comfortable and closed her eyes again. If she could just sleep for a couple more hours then she would feel fine, the effects of the booze would wear off. It always did.

At her back she felt something move and her eyes shot open.

She turned and saw that she wasn't alone in the bed. She opened her eyes wide and looked around. The room was small and untidy. There was a rail alongside the bed crammed with clothes and the beam of light came from the door which was ajar. It wasn't her bedroom.

Where was she?

She sat up. She was wearing just her pants and vest top. She rubbed her eyes and felt the crustiness of mascara that hadn't been taken off before she went to bed. She looked at the shape under the duvet beside her.

Who was it?

The tall lad who worked behind the bar?

The lad with the big earphones who bought that extra bottle of wine as the pub was closing? Or was it someone entirely different?

She slipped out of the bed and pulled her skirt and top on. She picked up her bag from the floor and walked barefoot across the room to the door. She peeked out into a hallway. The room was on the ground floor. The sun blazed in through the glass front door and she felt its warmth as she tiptoed across the hall looking for the toilet. There were three steps down to a long kitchen. She went there and stood for a moment looking round. The work surface was littered with empty beer cans and polystyrene dishes with a few remnants of uneaten chips. There was a wok on the cooker, its spoon still resting on the side. Dirty bowls sat nearby close to a half-empty bottle of vodka.

It was a student house. She'd seen enough of them.

She turned the tap on and rinsed a glass. Then she filled it with water and drank most of it down.

At the far end of the kitchen was a door and she pushed it open into a small bathroom. She used the toilet and stood at the sink to wash her hands. Looking at herself in the mirror she saw that her eye make-up was smudged underneath, making her look like a Goth. Most of her hair was still up in a ponytail but huge strands of it had fallen down at the sides and the back. She looked a wreck.

She thought back to the evening before. Saturday night. Why had she got so drunk? Then it came to her. It was because of the drowned girl.

When she headed out for the evening there had been a lot of police on the esplanade. It had unnerved her seeing the cars pulling up and screeching away, police officers walking with purpose, holding phones to their ears. Even though the child had gone missing at Sandy Bay the police seemed to be searching all the way along the seafront right up to the harbour and the ferry point. Dismayed, Kate had turned her back on it and hurried away, walking towards the outskirts of the town. There was a pub she'd gone to a few times over the last year. It had a garden and the booze was cheap. At the weekends it was always noisy and crowded and there were always lots of people to talk to and drink with.

She'd spent most of the evening there and somehow she'd ended up here in some stranger's house.

A whole night had passed. She wondered if the child's body had surfaced.

She peeled off some toilet paper, wet it and tried to get the make-up off from under her eyes. Then she pulled the tie out of her hair and rummaged in her make-up bag to search for a comb. Instead she found the small packet of condoms that she kept there. It was still covered in cellophane. Unused.

Who was it that she'd spent the night with? She stood very still for a moment and tried hard to remember. The tall lad behind the bar had been making eye contact with her all evening. *Do you fancy a drink after we close?* he'd said to her, when she went up to buy some beers. *Maybe*, she'd said, blowing him a kiss. The lad with the earphones had been cheeky. He'd come over to her when she was with the others and insisted he sat next to her, making other people budge up. He bought her a drink and rested the earphones on his collar. Then, when people in the pub headed off back to someone's house he bought a bottle of wine from behind the bar and they had followed along. From time to time she felt the touch of his fingers on her arm and when they got to the house he stuck with her. Then the lad from the bar had turned up. They all watched a film but there'd been a lot of wine and someone was smoking dope and rest of the evening just faded into blackness for her.

Was this the house? Or had they gone on somewhere else?

She splashed her face with water. Then she returned through the kitchen and crept back into the bedroom. She looked round, her eyes becoming accustomed to the darkness. It had once been someone's living room but like a lot of the houses in this area it had been turned into a bedroom. There was a bay window with blinds which cut out most of the light. On the floor, up against a wall, were piles of DVDs and CDs. Hundreds of them. In the bay window was a desk with an open laptop. There were books on it and on top of one of them was a pair of headphones. She smiled. That solved the mystery. Maybe it would be nice if she could remember his name. Bob? Steve? Or Tony? But maybe one of those belonged to the tall guy behind the bar.

She walked into the room and looked for her shoes. They were underneath the bed and she squatted down and pulled them out. She put them on and looked around in case she'd left anything else. A jacket or cardi? Had she been wearing one? It had been warm last night, she remembered that much.

She made her way quietly to the door.

There was movement from behind her. She stood very still. If he was just turning over she might still get away without any conversation.

"Hi," a voice said, huskily.

She turned round. He was sitting up, his chest pale in the darkened room.

"Would you pull one of the blinds up?"

She stepped over to the window and pulled on one of the roller blinds so that the sun trickled into the room and lightened it enough to see around.

"You're not going?" he said.

"I have to," she said. "I've got to see someone."

"Where do you live?"

"Near. Fifteen minutes' walk."

"But you don't have to go right this minute. I could get dressed, walk you home?"

"No, don't worry. I can make my own way. Like I said, I've got someone to see."

"Can I have your number?" he said.

"I don't know."

"Go on. I'll give you a call. We can get a drink or a bite to eat."

She didn't answer. She could just walk out. It wouldn't be rude. She hardly knew him. He sat up though, his legs swinging out of the bed. She looked away, afraid that he might be naked. He picked his phone off the floor and held it out at her. She couldn't refuse it. She took it and stood over by the light, pressing buttons, feeding her number into his phone. She put her name, *Kate*, in. Then she handed it back.

"I'll give you mine, if you like."

She couldn't be unkind. She got her phone out of her bag and handed it to him. He took a moment to do it and stood up to hand it back. He was wearing boxers and she must have been looking at them oddly.

"We didn't… you know… last night," he said.

"Oh."

"You were pretty drunk. You needed a long sleep. But I did undress you. Just your top things. I thought you'd be more comfortable. That was all right, wasn't it?"

"Sure."

"Got a hangover?"

"Not really. Well. A little bit."

"You could come and lie down again. It's early yet."

She smiled and shook her head. "I told you. I've got to go."

"See you, Kate."

She nodded.

"You don't even know my name, do you?"

"I do!" she said.

"What is it?"

He was calling her bluff. She simply couldn't remember it. She picked her phone out of her pocket and looked down her list of contacts and came across the most recently entered name.

"Jimmy Fuller."

He smiled. "Remember me, now."

"See you," she said.

She walked out of the room and out of the house. It took her a moment to work out where she was. The street was unfamiliar so she walked along it until she came to a junction. Then she saw the pub she'd been in the previous evening. She went on. It was another sunny day and she screwed her eyes up as she went.

When she got closer to the beach she listened for any sirens but it was silent. She was still thirsty so she went into a shop and bought a bottle of water. The woman who served her was talking on her phone and Kate waited patiently until she'd finished her conversation, then handed over her money.

"Any news on the girl who drowned?" she said.

The woman nodded but made a face. "They found her late last night. Only she didn't drown. She was murdered."

FIVE

Kate went straight up to her bedroom. Her mind was racing. The little girl's body had been found. Not drowned but *murdered*. The news made her feel wretched.

Her room was messy from the night before when she had rushed out. Her work skirt was sitting on the floor where she had dropped it. She picked it up and brushed it down. There was a pile of ironing there, waiting for her to work her way through it. She sighed. The house was quiet. There was no sound from Ruth's room. No doubt Robbie was with her. It was gone eleven and the pair didn't usually surface till the afternoon on Sundays. She couldn't hear anything from Sally's room either.

She noticed a large padded envelope on her bedside table with a Post-it stuck to it. It was Sally's handwriting.

This came for you today. You must have missed it on the hall table XXX

She picked the envelope up and opened it. A piece of paper came out, and a paperback book. She held onto the paper but her eyes were drawn to the book. *Children Who Kill, by Sara Wright*. The words underneath the title made her breath catch in her throat. *The Case of Jennifer Jones*.

She sat down on the bed, shaken. *Sara Wright*. She recognised the name. Sara Wright was the journalist who had tricked her way into her life. Kate flicked through the book. One hundred and ninety-two pages. How could anyone write that much about her and what she had done?

She unfolded the paper. It was a letter from Jill Newton, her first probation officer.

Dear Kate,

I hope you are well. This was sent to me a couple of weeks ago to be passed onto you. It is just being published, I understand. I kept it because I honestly didn't know whether to forward it or not. I know it will upset you. However, I read it myself and I have to say it is a well-written and sympathetic piece of work. Sara Wright, for all her questionable methods, has written a decent book and I doubt that it will do you any harm. Of course, the media will be reviewing this book or writing about its publication and I would guess that you might be upset if those kind of articles surface again. But the book itself is well meaning, I believe. This is why I've sent it to you. I hope you are enjoying your degree.

Yours,
Jill Newton

Kate opened the book. There was a foreword. She read it over.

A year or so ago, while working as a newspaper reporter, I followed up a story about the release of Jennifer Jones, the child who had killed her friend at a nature park six years before. I had information that this girl was living in Croydon with a carer. In order to find out how she was adjusting to life, living with a false identity, I worked undercover, befriending the girl's carer and observing the girl living an ordinary life. My aim had been to eventually persuade the girl to trust me and be interviewed by our newspaper, to let the public see the human side of this girl. I also intended to write a book about the case. Unfortunately before this could take place her identity was compromised and she had to relocate. I never did interview Jennifer Jones, but my account of her early days of freedom in Croydon is based on my personal experience. I have done extensive investigation into the killing at Berwick Waters, the families concerned and the immediate aftermath.

My aim for this book is to add to the sum of human understanding about children and crime.

Sara Wright

Kate let the book drop onto the bed. Then she picked it up and walked across to the chest of drawers. She placed it in a drawer, covering it with a tangle of clothes. Not now. She did not want to read it now. She might never want to read it.

She had a shower and put on fresh clothes. Then she went

downstairs to the kitchen. It was a complete contrast to the one she had just left in the student house. It was clean and tidy, the surfaces clear apart from a few jars and a toaster. The dishes were stacked away, the cutlery was in the right compartments in the right drawers, the mugs were hanging on hooks and the tea towel was folded over the rack. The orderliness of it made her feel calm.

Kate knew how lucky she had been to get a room in this house. Both Sally and Ruth were older than her, both working in local jobs. Each of them was reasonably tidy and neither of them had *ever* taken any of her stuff without asking. She'd met them four months before when her previous rental agreement ran out. She'd been keen to move out of Exeter, away from the student world she'd lived exclusively in for two years. Julia Masters had been helpful, for a change. She'd told her that a friend of a friend was moving out of her house and so there was a place free. *Don't worry*, Julia had said. *It's not a work friend of mine so they know nothing about who you are.* Kate had seen the house, noted the sea view and the fact that Sally and Ruth were so mature and yet friendly. She'd been tired of living in student houses and wanted the room straight away but she sensed they weren't sure. She still had another year of university left to do and she wondered if they thought she'd be inviting lots of friends around and having parties. When she phoned, Sally said that there were other people who had to look at it first. She felt it slipping away from her so one evening she'd gone round and knocked on the door and presented Ruth with a tin of homemade biscuits that she'd cooked that afternoon. *I'm not trying to influence your decision*, she'd said, *this is just a gift*. The next day Sally called and said she could have the room. One night when they'd had a few drinks Sally told her that it wasn't to do with the biscuits as such; it was the fact that she wanted the room *that much*.

Kate opened the cupboard with her name on it and took out some bread and a pot of jam. She unhooked a mug and put the kettle on. When she'd made her toast she sat down at the table. The arrival of the book came into her head and she tried to shake it away. The sound of footsteps on the stairs distracted her. A few moments later Sally came into the kitchen. She had a long dressing gown on, and her hair was tousled.

"Morning," she said, her voice scratchy.

"Hi," Kate said. "Sorry, did I wake you?"

Sally shook her head. "Been awake for a while. In any case I'm going to see Mum and Dad today. Get your parcel?"

Kate nodded and drank her tea. Sally seemed a little brusque.

"Anything wrong?" Kate said, but as she spoke she remembered rushing out the previous evening, even though Sally had offered to cook.

"Where were you last night? Remember, last time, when you stayed out? You said you'd send a text if you weren't coming home?"

"Sorry."

"God! No, I'm sorry. I feel like a mother hen," Sally said.

"You fed up with me?"

Kate frowned. She *liked* Sally worrying about her. It reminded her of when she lived with Rosie, in Croydon, after she was first released.

"Course not. Well, only when you're being a kitchen freak.

Crumbs on the work surface is not a hanging offence, Kate. Putting the pots back in the cupboard in the wrong order won't bring about the end of the world. Loosen up!"

"Ouch."

"I'm joking. I like having you around."

"Is Robbie upstairs with Ruth?"

"Does the night follow day? Course he is. Are you going to make me some tea?"

"Toast?"

"Only with your jam, not that horrible shop stuff."

"It's not so bad me being a kitchen freak then?"

"I suppose not. Just send a text next time you stay out all night, OK? Who was he?"

"Who?"

"The guy."

"No one you know."

"Question is, did *you* know him?"

Kate didn't answer.

Later, when Sally had gone upstairs to get dressed, Kate washed the breakfast things up at the sink. While she did so she looked out at the tiny back garden, just a square of grass with some pot plants around the edge. The garden next door was bigger and had a child's climbing frame in it. Kate craned her neck to see if any of the neighbour's children were out in the garden, but they weren't. Then she saw the pink ball that had come over the fence and was perched like a boiled egg on top of one of Sally's pots.

Lucy Bussell came into her head again. Kate wondered if Lucy was mentioned in the *book*. Lucy would be sixteen now

41

but Kate only had an image of a small, thin, grubby child. Lucy Bussell's clothes had always been too big for her and she had worn the same things day after day. Kate wondered what she was like now. When Kate was ten, that summer (when she was *Jennifer*), she had called her *Mouse*. It had been an unkind thing to do.

She dried her hands and folded the tea towel up again. She went back up to her room and stood by the window looking out to the sea. She wondered *how* Lucy had received the letter she had sent her. She tried to picture the girl; a college student, tall, still thin, her hair longer perhaps. She only knew the child though so it was hard for her to get a face in her head.

Kate remembered the day she found Lucy's address.

It was weeks before during a session in Julia Masters' office. Julia was not there and Kate was being interviewed by a woman from Bristol University, someone who Julia knew. The woman's name was Barbara something and she was researching *The Consequences of Crime* for her PhD in Criminology. Barbara was working with a number of people, offenders and victims. None of them would be identified in the study.

They were sitting either side of Julia's desk. Barbara had a book open on the work surface and was writing Kate's answers down. She was doing it slowly as if recording every single word. Kate had to repeat herself a couple of times. From time to time Barbara glanced at her phone which was alongside the book.

It rang and she jumped slightly, as though it was the last thing she expected.

"I'm so sorry, Kate. I absolutely have to get this. It's my son's school. I'll take it outside."

She pulled a diary from her bag and left the office.

Kate looked at Barbara's bag. It was spilling its contents out on Julia's neat desk. She had an urge to right it, tidy it, but then saw the corner of a piece of paper sticking out of a file. The name *Lucy Alexander (Bussell)* was printed on it. It gave her a jolt. She pulled it out of the bag and read the name again and saw that there was also an address in London and an email address.

She stared at the piece of paper in her hand.

It was like a window opening onto her past.

From outside the door she heard the sound of Barbara's voice. She could come back in any minute and see Kate with the piece of paper and it might look as though she had been rifling through her things. Kate felt a moment's panic. She should put it back, tuck it into the file from which it had slipped. Close it off.

She took a pen out of her bag and grabbed a Post-it from Julia's desk. She quickly copied the address down. Then she replaced the piece of paper in the file.

Barbara came back into the room

"Sorry about that, Kate. Where were we?"

The interview continued. The Post-it sat in Kate's pocket like a tiny ticking bomb.

Lucy Bussell's address; like a hand reaching out to her.

SIX

On Monday Kate had the afternoon off work. She spent it ironing and making some bread. While she kneaded the dough she had her phone on the side and found herself looking at it from time to time. She'd half expected a message from Jimmy Fuller, a quick text that said something like, *Fancy a drink?* Or *Come round to ours?* Or *Good to meet you on Saturday.* It had happened before. Boys who she'd hooked up with, spent the night with, they were often keen to see her again. She knew why, she knew they thought her an easy conquest.

In the last two years there had been many such boys. She'd even spent a bit of time with some of them. Boys who followed football teams, who wore this year's football shirt and talked about their players like gods or devils. There were also the boys who loved to be fit; who spent the week running or cycling and then spent the weekend in the university bar. She'd even liked the studious boys, who read books while they were having their lunch and talked about poetry and culture.

She liked the feel of these boys, the hardness of their backs and their shoulders. She liked the heat of them, the fervour of their kisses, the excited rush they always seemed to be in.

She smiled at their untidy rooms and tiptoed across a sea of clothes and books, taking care not to kick over a cup or glass that had been discarded earlier. She slipped into their unmade beds and didn't mind the crumbs and the socks that sometimes surfaced. She gave over her packet of condoms and in return she held onto these boys and felt them shiver and stiffen. Afterwards they fell into a deep sleep and woke up full of passion again. But she always stole away, gathering her clothes up in handfuls, searching for her bag and her shoes, getting dressed in the corner of the room or the bathroom.

When she saw them in college she was amazed at their shyness or embarrassment. They didn't make eye contact and mumbled that they'd meant to ring her and she smiled and tried to put them at their ease. Then there were those who acted differently, with cockiness. It was as if they had conned her in some way and when she saw them they seemed to whisper to their friends and eye her warily as if she'd loaned them some money and was looking for payment. But she'd had what she wanted from them and she gave them a wave and moved on.

There were a few she'd seen over and over but it was always on a casual basis. She didn't like making arrangements. It was always better to bump into them in the university bar or one of the pubs near the student houses that she'd lived in. Then it was up to her whether or not she stayed with them.

Sometimes, after one of these nights, she thought of Frankie, her first boyfriend. He'd been a college student in Croydon and one evening, after leaving work, she'd been amazed to see him standing in the street waiting for her. He'd walked along the road with her and told her about himself and asked her what she was doing serving people cups of coffee all day. She'd told him she was on a gap year; that had been her backstory, the explanation for her lifestyle. *I thought people were supposed to do their gap year in Africa, not Croydon!* he'd joked and somehow his arm had crept round her shoulder. When they got to the door of Rosie's flat he'd kissed her so hard it had made her head spin. After that they were together and she'd loved being with him. He was big and muscular and she felt safe with him. He had told her he loved her but when things got difficult he hadn't loved her enough. So it was easier to spend time with frivolous boys who didn't make any demands on her; nice boys with soft hands and a pocket full of chatter. These boys were easy to find. Jimmy Fuller was one such boy.

The front doorbell sounded. The harsh ring broke into her thoughts. She quickly plonked the mass of dough into a bowl and laid a damp cloth across it.

"Coming," she shouted, walking along the hall, drying her fingers with a tea towel.

A man and woman, smartly dressed, were standing at the front door. The man was moving from one foot to the other as if nervous about something.

"Kate Rickman?" he said.

Kate nodded.

"You're *Kate Rickman*?" he said. "I thought you'd be taller."

"Get on with it, Simon," the woman said.

Kate frowned. She had a bad feeling about these people.

"Right. *Kate*," he said, enunciating her name so that it sounded odd. "I am Detective Constable Simon Kelsey and this is Detective Constable Pat Knight."

They both showed ID cards.

"We would like you to come with us to Exeter police station to answer some questions regarding the disappearance of Jodie Mills."

"Jodie Mills?"

For a second Kate had no idea what they were talking about. Then the name rang a bell. *Jodie Mills*. The nine-year-old-girl who everyone thought had drowned. She'd been murdered though; the woman in the shop had told her.

"There are just a few things that we'd like to clear up."

"But why me? I don't know her, I've never seen her."

"If you'd just come, we have the car here and I'm sure we can do this quietly without friends or neighbours seeing anything."

"Wait. No, I won't. I can't. I don't know why you want to question me…" Kate edged behind the door as if shielding herself.

"Show her," DC Simon Kelsey said, exhaling.

DC Knight produced a piece of paper. On it was a photograph. For a second Kate thought she was looking at a picture of Jodie Mills. But then she looked again. It was a photocopy of a picture of a young girl, but it wasn't Jodie Mills. It was *her*. Her when she was Jennifer Jones, when she appeared in newspaper articles, her face staring out of the front pages. The headline was faded but still shocking. JJ: FACE OF A KILLER.

"So you see, miss," DC Kelsey said, "it would be better if you came quietly. That way no one gets to know your little secret."

He gave her an unpleasant smile. Kate glared at him. He stared back, his eyes ice blue. His hair was gelled so that it stood in spikes at the front. The other DC was looking down at her shoes.

"I don't think you can do this…" she mumbled.

"*Jennifer Jones*," he whispered, loudly, "I can arrest you or you can come of your own free will. The choice is yours."

Kate stuttered out something about getting her bag and meeting them at the car. They walked off and she closed the front door and felt faint against it. *How dare they! What right did he have to speak to her like that?*

Kate walked back into the kitchen. She had to stay calm. This might turn out to be nothing. And the bread was only half made. She grabbed a notepad and wrote on it, *Bread proving. Gone out for a couple of hours. Kate.* Her handwriting was all over the place but at least she'd left a note.

When she went upstairs to get her bag and phone, her hand was trembling. She picked up the hairbrush and looked out of the window at a silver car further along the road. The male DC was leaning against it, smoking a cigarette. The female DC was talking on her phone and glanced up at Kate's window.

Why hadn't she considered it? She pulled the brush roughly through her hair. How had it not occurred to her? A child is murdered in the middle of a community where a convicted killer is living.

She would be a suspect.

She flung the brush down and stood very still, trying to calm herself.

Then she went out of the house and headed for the police car.

SEVEN

Kate sat in the back of the police car as the countryside flew by. Her bag was scrunched up on her lap. She stared out of the window, her throat tight as if something was squeezing it.

"Where exactly are we going?" she said, after a while.

"Middlemoor, Exeter. Thought you'd be happier away from your home ground," DC Kelsey said. "Save anyone you know seeing you. Putting two and two together, Kate. Or would you rather I call you *Jennifer*. I don't mind. After all we, the police, are at your service."

"No need to be sarcastic, Simon," DC Knight said.

"Just stating it like it is, Pat. Does this lady wish to be called by her proper name, that's all I'm asking. Miss Jennifer Jones? What's wrong with that? It's the name she was born with."

"My name is Kate."

She said it quietly. She was confused. She wasn't sure why he was speaking to her like this. It was as if he knew her and hated her. She crossed her legs and folded her arms and stared out at the road. She thought of ringing Julia Masters and telling her what was happening. DC Kelsey had told her she was free to make a call if she wished when she got into the car. Indeed Julia herself had explained the protocol of what to do should she ever be involved with the police, *If you get accused of something, shoplifting for example or drug crime, you give the officers my name and number.* She'd looked at Julia as though she was mad. Why would she ever shoplift? Or buy drugs?

That's why she hadn't rung her. She was nineteen years old. She could be interviewed on her own. She'd done nothing wrong. There was no reason why Julia Masters should even know she'd been with the police.

"So, what's it like? Being so famous?" DC Kelsey said. "Or *infamous* is perhaps a better word. I heard that you'd get pots of money if you told your story to the newspapers."

DC Knight looked round at her, waiting for a response. Kate stared back at the police officer. What could she possibly say to these officers to make them less vile?

"She doesn't say much, does she?" he went on. "Probably got a load of solicitors lined up ready to sue the police."

"You shouldn't go on. She might make a complaint," DC Knight said.

"About what? I'm just chatting. Just passing the time of day."

Kate closed her eyes. If she could just ignore his ugly words.

"In any case, it's her word against mine."

They drove on in silence until they reached the outskirts of Exeter. Kate recognised the streets from the previous year when she'd lived there as a student. She was gripping her bag and wondered whether she *should* ring Julia Masters. The hostility she was getting from this police officer was making her feel fearful.

DC Knight turned round again. Her voice was softer.

"How long have you lived in Exmouth?"

"Just a few months," Kate said. "I lived in Exeter for the first two years of my degree."

"You work for tourist information?"

"It's just a summer job."

The woman was being friendly. At least it seemed that way. Just then Kate remembered something that Jill Newton had said to her. *Don't ever give away too much of yourself, Alice, you never know what people's intentions are.* Her name had been *Alice* then; not Jennifer, not Kate.

"Got a boyfriend?"

Kate frowned and turned her face away from the woman.

"No point in being nice to her, Pat. She's a suspect in a murder investigation. Course, it's not new for you is it, Jennifer. You've been in this position before."

"I don't have to talk to you," she muttered.

"She knows her rights," said DC Knight.

They were pulling into a parking space. Kate hadn't noticed that they'd arrived at the police station. The car pulled up sharply and the handbrake creaked. She turned to get out but felt the young detective's stare.

"The thing is, Jennifer, I spend my days trying to catch criminals. And you know what happens to them? They get a smart barrister and get off. Or if they do get time they get out early because of overcrowding or good behaviour or some such…"

"Leave it, Simon," DC Knight said.

"And then, on top of that, when a particularly unpleasant

51

killer is released they get a new identity. And you know who pays for it? Taxpayers. While you're being protected, looked after by your social worker, your probation officer, your counsellor, police stations are closing and officers are being made redundant. While you're taking your degree and," he put his fingers in the air to indicate inverted commas, "'Putting your life back together' we're paying for it!"

Kate felt her resolve slipping. Her throat was filling up. There was absolute loathing in this man's eyes. She tried the door handle but it was locked.

"Oops sorry, central locking," DC Kelsey said, pressing a switch.

The door opened and she stumbled out. She was definitely going to ring Julia Masters. She wasn't going to put up with this harassment. She strode towards the entrance and then stopped in her tracks. She could hear the police officers coming behind her, their voices light as if they were just passing the time of day.

Julia Masters was standing inside the doors of the police station.

She knew then that there had never been any need to call Julia. Julia already knew she had been brought in. Maybe it was Julia, herself, who arranged it.

The interview room was surprisingly large. She looked round and saw pinboards and a couple of fold-up chairs against the wall. The table in front of her had a bottle of water and a glass. There was recording equipment and a pad with pens by the side. Julia was sitting next to her.

A woman came into the room accompanied by DC Knight. Kate stared at her. She was tall and thin, wearing a dark trouser suit with a pale blue shirt. Her hair was pulled back and she had no make-up on.

"I'm Detective Inspector Lauren Heart. You've already met my colleague. Now let's get the formalities out of the way."

She explained to Kate that she wasn't under arrest and that she didn't have to answer questions if she didn't want to, that she could leave any time. Kate knew this but felt immobile. She couldn't have got out of the chair if she'd wanted to. She stared at a large ring the inspector had on. It was silver and garnet, the stone dark red, almost black. She registered that DI Heart was addressing her as *Kate* and not referring to her birth name. It made her warm to the detective, nodding her head politely to show that she was paying attention. The detective explained about the recording equipment and then started the interview.

"Now, Kate, can you tell us where you were on Friday evening?"

Kate paused. "I left work, went home then went out for a swim."

"What time did you go for a swim?"

"About seven. Just before seven."

"A little late to go swimming?"

"It was a hot evening. I'd been at work all day and was just winding down. I love to swim."

Kate glanced at Julia as if she wanted her to confirm this fact. Julia was staring straight ahead.

"Where did you go?"

53

"Sandy Bay. I got the bus and headed up there. I like that beach better than…"

A grim feeling was building up inside her. Pieces of a puzzle seemed to drop into place inside her head. This wasn't just some routine interview. She was at Sandy Bay on the same night the little girl got killed.

"So you spent, what? An hour swimming? On the beach?"

"Give or take. Maybe a bit longer."

"What time did you leave the beach?

"I don't know, exactly. Maybe seven thirty or nearer to eight."

"You went home?"

"No, I walked up the coastal path to the top and sat and watched the sun go down."

"Where?"

"On top of the cliffs. It's actually a place that's fenced off? But there's a way through and I sit near the top. It's a… It's a great view."

"What did you do? When you were sitting watching the sun go down?"

"I read a bit of my book. I don't know, I just sat and thought about stuff. I had had a tiring day."

Kate's voice was rising.

DI Heart sat back and looked at Kate for what seemed like a long time. Kate glanced at Julia who gave her a reassuring nod, as if to say, *you're doing well!* Kate didn't respond. She sat erect in her chair and pushed Julia out of her field of vision. It was no good her being nice now. Julia had delivered her here, like a ready-packaged chicken.

"Can I ask why I've been brought here?" Kate said. "Why you're asking me these questions?"

"You were seen on the coastal path about ten, Kate. Someone saw you walking along. You were recognised. A witness said they saw one of the girls from the tourist information centre."

"I *was* there. That's not a secret."

"Are you aware, Kate, that the body of Jodie Mills was found late last night?"

"I only heard this morning that she had been murdered. I don't know any more than that. I thought she had drowned."

"I'm afraid not. She was found in the undergrowth some metres from the coastal path."

There was a moment's silence and Kate found herself holding her breath. She had no idea what was going to be said. She steeled herself.

"May I ask you some things, Kate, about your past?"

DI Heart looked a little embarrassed. Her past had already been referred to in the car but DI Heart wasn't to know that. Kate focused on the police officer's ring. One minute it looked black, the next it was red. It was sombre, heavy. The detective's finger didn't look strong enough to hold it.

"You know it all already," Kate said.

"The details, yes. You and two other girls went up to a local beauty spot called Berwick Waters in May eight years ago. While there you pushed one of the girls into the lake and hit the other one with a baseball bat."

Kate crossed her arms tightly. It was bald, it was brief, but it told the facts as they were. She couldn't deny it. There was so much more to be said though but the words were boxed away in her head. DI Heart was looking at her enquiringly; giving her a chance to answer, to soften the story if she could.

But her mouth wouldn't open and the room seemed to tilt away from her. She grabbed the edge of the table for support.

"I didn't mean to push Lucy into the lake," she said. "I *did* push her but she wasn't supposed…"

"This girl, Lucy Bussell, ran away, and you attempted to bury the other girl even though she was still alive?"

The timbre of DI Heart's voice rose on the last words *even though she was still alive.*

"I didn't realise," Kate said, looking down at her lap, her voice dropping. "Of course, I thought the worst. I was a child. I had no idea… I thought she was gone."

"You didn't tell any adults about this? As soon as it happened, I mean."

Kate had a fleeting image in her head of the adult in her life. Her mother, Carol Jones, one-time model for fashion catalogues turned glamour model. Her sweet smiling mother who would take her clothes off for the promise of a photo in a magazine. Kate felt a pain in her chest, a twist of her heart.

"No."

"As I understand it, you never gave any explanation for this behaviour?"

Kate shook her head, the enormity of the question too much for her. No explanation was possible.

"Well, Kate. You need to see it from our point of view. You'll perhaps understand that when we found the body of a young girl with a head injury we did everything we could to find out what happened. We made enquiries and were told that one of the people who had been seen close to the spot where the body was found was a girl who worked for the local tourist information office. That girl had a violent past and was living with a new identity. This is why we are so keen to question her."

Kate looked at Julia. Had she volunteered the information? Or had the police gone to her?

"Did you see or speak to this young girl on Friday evening?"

Kate shook her head, angry now. "You're asking me this because of something I did when I was ten years old?"

"Partly. But there is more."

Kate frowned, puzzled.

"The police were told that the victim, Jodie Mills, had gone swimming. The initial search for her took place around the water and along the shore. It was only on Saturday morning, more than twelve hours after she went missing, that we began to search the general area of Sandy Bay. Her body was discovered later that day. She was fully dressed. When her clothes were examined we found something very interesting. In the pocket of her jeans was a badge shaped like a teddy bear. It was a tourist office badge and it had your name on it, Kate."

"What?"

"How did your badge get into the pocket of the dead girl, Kate?"

Kate had no answer.

EIGHT

Kate was sitting in the passenger seat of Julia's car, which was parked behind the police station. In her hand she had a tissue which she was shredding. She stared out of the window. Julia was standing by the exit doors making a phone call, no doubt checking that her sons, Justin and Peter, were OK. A police car was idling nearby, blocking the lane as a uniformed officer emerged from the building and jumped into the car, hardly closing the door before it shot off.

If Kate had been a smoker she would have had a cigarette.

Instead she bunched up the shreds of tissue and shoved them into her pocket.

DI Heart had been called from the interview on a pressing matter so they had been told to go home and wait to be called back into the station for more questions. Kate had walked from the room in a daze. In her head had been an image of the teddy bear badge that had been found in Jodie Mills' jeans pocket. Kate remembered it. Aimee had wanted them to wear these badges so that the shop seemed more child friendly; teddy bears, monkeys, dogs, tigers. Her name had been printed under it in a child-friendly font, *Kate*.

Julia got back into the car and started the engine.

"Let's get going," she said, brusquely.

As the car pulled out of the car park Kate wondered where DC Simon Kelsey was. Was he regaling other officers with his story about picking up Jennifer Jones? *I told her what I thought of all this new identity rubbish!* She looked back at the windows of the station. There were only a couple and they were opaque. At least he hadn't been grinning down at her. What would he say when he heard that Kate's badge had been in the pocket of the dead girl? Perhaps he already knew. Maybe that was why he had been so nasty to her.

How had the badge got there? The question made Kate feel panicky. How could it be explained?

Her phone vibrated and she took it out of her pocket. It was a text from Sally.

What am I supposed to do with this bread?

It was gone six. Sally was home from work. No doubt Ruth and Robbie were there too. They would be wondering why she hadn't finished baking the bread as she'd said she would. She tapped out a message.

Bake the bread at 220C for 30 mins then let it rest on a tray x

She left it at that. Sally would just think she'd gone to a pub somewhere.

The drive back was slow, the evening traffic stopping and starting as it headed out of Exeter.

"It'll be all right," Julia said. "There'll be some explanation for the badge."

"It's not just about the badge though, is it? It's because of what I did when I was ten years old."

"This is just normal procedure for the police. Talking to you is just a box-ticking exercise for them."

"Except for the badge," she said.

The badge; since working at the tourist information centre she had had a couple of new badges every week. They were made of card but they weren't robust. They creased and flopped and eventually looked grotty.

"I am telling the truth."

"Of course you are, Kate. I never doubted it."

"Was it you who told the police about me?"

"They have their own databases of known criminals," Julia said, clearing her throat.

Known criminal. That's what Kate was.

"They contacted me. I thought you might need a friendly face there, that's why I went along."

Now she felt guilty for misjudging Julia.

She'd been judged though. For something she hadn't done. She'd been subjected to an interrogation. She felt a deep sense of injustice and yet she, Kate Rickman, had no right to remonstrate. She had a record involving violence against another child. She'd been in the area at the time Jodie Mills was killed. Something of hers was found on the child. The police would have been failing in their duty if they hadn't picked her up.

It didn't make her feel any better.

Julia dropped her off near the esplanade.

"I can walk from here," she said.

"Call me if you hear from the police again. If I'm free I'll come with you."

Kate nodded and watched the car drive off, Julia reaching across to turn on the radio as she went, clearly already forgetting about Kate and her troubles.

She didn't know what to do. If she went home, Ruth and Sally would be there, chatty and relaxed, and she couldn't imagine herself sitting down to a meal, laughing about the uncooked bread, keeping the details of her afternoon to herself. Neither did she want to go up to her room and sit by herself. She needed to be out, in the air, near the sea, and yet she couldn't face the beach.

She walked off towards the docks. When she got there it was busy, the bars and restaurants packed with customers, most sitting at tables outside. Some people were lounging on decks of boats, some idling along the dock, looking at maps and talking to boat owners.

The docks were not her favourite place. The seawater looked black and the boats seemed to crowd the marina, like a shopping centre car park. Everything was concrete and sharp edges and the people there were dressed up to the nines. They talked loudly and looked like they were shopping for things; drinks, partners, boats, status. The beach was such a contrast. People seemed relaxed there, watching the water edge up to the land and slip away again. Even adults played in the sea and the sand, regardless of how foolish they made themselves look. The beach was a soft place. She looked round at the crowds, faces caked with make-up and hard young men posing at the edges of the tables, and she was reminded of DI Simon Kelsey. She pictured him standing there, a bottle of beer in his hand, talking loudly to anyone who would listen. *So this ex-con is taking her degree and 'Putting her life back together' and we're paying for it!*

She decided to go home.

"Hi, Kate!" a voice said.

She turned round.

It was the boy whose bed she'd slept in on Saturday, Jimmy Fuller. He was wearing jeans and a sleeveless T-shirt and carrying a bag over his shoulder.

"What you doing here?" he said.

"I was just… I was just walking. You?"

"I was just passing through. I came off the ferry. I've got a mate who lives over there."

He hooked his thumb in the direction of the Starcross ferry terminal.

"I'm glad I've seen you," he went on. "I was going to give you a call later."

For a second he seemed to falter. Then he put his hand in his pocket and pulled something out. His held his palm out to her. In it was a gold chain with a flat heart pendant.

"You left this behind. I found it in my bed."

He whispered the words *in my bed*.

She took it from him. It had been given to her in a previous life by Frankie. She'd recently started to wear it again. She hadn't noticed that it was gone.

"The chain is broken. You can have it fixed though. The odd thing is that it's got a name engraved on it, *Alice*. I wasn't sure if it was yours."

Kate looked at the letters. They were in italics, soft on the eye.

"So, is it yours?" Jimmy said.

"Why?" she said, smiling. "Might you have had a girl called *Alice* sleeping in your bed during the last week?"

She took the chain and tucked it into her jeans pocket.

"I only allow one strange girl a week in my bed."

"Good rule of thumb that. Thanks for the pendant. I must go though. I've got some bread proving at home."

"You make bread?" he said, looking at her with surprise.

"I do. I'm a good cook."

"So am I!" he said. "Why don't you come back to mine. I was planning to make some food."

"Any homemade bread?"

"No, but I've got other things that will make up for that."

"Well, in that case," she said.

"So what do I call you?" Jimmy said, as they walked away from the docks. "Kate or Alice?"

"Kate. Definitely."

NINE

The kitchen had improved. There were no dirty dishes anywhere and most of the work surface had been tidied. Jimmy gave her a cold beer from the fridge and unpacked the bag he'd had with him. He placed a pile of DVD box sets on the kitchen table.

"This guy I know in Starcross? He's a big crime fan as well and we swap."

Kate let her eye run over the box sets. One crime series after another. A couple she recognised from television but most she'd never heard of.

"Classic US crime drama. Some of these are hard to get hold of," he said.

"Is this what you're doing your MA in?"

"No! Early twentieth-century literature."

"Oh. Sounds heavy." It wasn't what she'd expected him to say.

"Not really. It's all about shaking off the shackles of the Victorians and coping with the new century. Social and cultural changes. And then there's the coming war."

Kate felt a moment's envy. During her first year at university she'd become immersed in early twentieth-century history and had decided that she would do an MA on *The Growth of Feminism in the Pre-War Years*. She'd thought about it for months and even spoke to her tutor about it but somewhere, during the last year, the interest seemed to slip away.

A half-dressed young man suddenly appeared. He mumbled something and walked through heading for the bathroom, a giant towel over his shoulder. Just then loud music came from above as well as the sound of doors banging.

"That's Tony," Jimmy said, pointing up to the ceiling. "And that was Col going into the bathroom."

"Just three of you live here?"

"There was a fourth. Becky, my ex-girlfriend. She moved out a couple of months ago. It's OK. I was upset at the time but I'm fine now."

"Right."

"She's involved in a six-month archaeology project on some island north of Scotland. We've sublet her room to Karen, a girl who's down here for the summer. She has a job in one of the gift shops. But Becky will be coming back at Christmas. I'm looking after some of her stuff."

"But it's over between you."

"Definitely. Over. Just good friends. Now I'm going to make stir fry," he said. "This is a five-star recipe."

"Really?"

"I know what you're thinking," Jimmy said. "Because I'm male I can't cook."

"No, not at all."

"Cooking is important to me. I never buy ready meals. I make everything from scratch. No additives but proper ingredients."

Kate smiled at him. He was so earnest. He looked as though

65

he was waiting for her approval.

"Is something wrong? Are you laughing at me?"

"No."

"I'm not that good with girls. I haven't had much experience."

"You seemed pretty determined on Saturday night."

"But we didn't do anything. I told you..."

"I know. I didn't mean *that*. I meant in the pub. You stuck with me for a long time."

"Well... I.... I liked you... Actually, you don't remember but we did meet before. At a party in Exeter. I chatted to you for a while but you were a little drunk. Then you disappeared so..."

"I'm sorry, I don't remember ..."

"But you know me now!"

He busied himself cleaning the inside of the wok with paper towel and then started to chop vegetables. She thought about what he'd said about his ex-girlfriend. She'd gone to *some island* north of Scotland. Kate was certain that he knew the name of the island and maybe even her address off by heart. He was still hurting, she was sure. She felt a surge of sympathy for him.

"What about you? Where do you come from? Not round here, I can tell by your accent," he said.

"I'm from Norwich. My parents split and my mum remarried. I don't get on with my stepdad so I tend to stay round here in the holidays."

Kate said it off pat. She'd told many people versions of this history over the last two years.

"Do you still see your dad?"

Kate shook her head. It was the truth. She had never seen

66

her biological father.

"So you're on your own. Brothers? Sisters?"

"Just me. I'm happy that way. I have friends here. I'll probably stay here after I finish my degree."

He nodded and threw two handfuls of vegetables into the wok. It made a loud sizzling sound. It smelled good. She realised she was very hungry. She ran her fingers through her hair and felt the knots in it.

"I just need to brush my hair," she said, grabbing her bag, standing up.

"Col's in the bathroom. Use my room. It's pretty tidy."

She walked into Jimmy's bedroom. The blinds were up and the room was full of light. It looked much bigger than it had on Sunday morning. It was tidier but not tidy. The duvet had been straightened but there were still bumps in it, probably covering T-shirts or underwear that had been discarded. Boys *never* made their beds neatly. She sat down on the corner of the bed and angled her face so that she could see into a mirror that was on the wall. She pulled the brush through her hair, pausing when she got to the knots, teasing them out.

She realised she hadn't thought about the police for a while. It was all there in her head, the interrogation, the teddy bear badge, but it wasn't at the *front* of her mind. She felt *relaxed* and remembered Julia's words, *There'll be some explanation for the badge.* Maybe she was right.

Was she actually *enjoying* herself?

She shouldn't be feeling like this. At the very least this house should have depressed her. She'd had her fill of student houses and their chaos. The communal areas were the worst;

the grubby kitchens with their sticky floors, the hallways that got filled up with people's coats and bikes and shopping bags. That's why she loved it with Sally and Ruth. Theirs was a sane existence. Everything had a place and if there were coats over the newel post they would disappear in a few hours.

Jimmy Fuller's keenness should have worried her. He'd met her before and clearly remembered it. Perhaps that's why he had stuck with her on the previous Saturday night. And he had an ex-girlfriend whom he clearly still had feelings for.

He was someone who had big emotions. The sort of person she usually steered clear of. The odd thing was she liked him. He was good company and she felt easy with him.

And she was *attracted* to him. Why not? After the way she'd been treated. Why shouldn't she have a good time?

She looked around his room. The piles of DVDs seemed at a precarious angle; one knock and they would all come toppling down. Her eye settled on some plastic boxes in an alcove. Each had a label on the side with the word *Becky* written on it in felt tip pen. She went over to them and picked the lid off the top one, curious about this girl who had been close to Jimmy. The box was full of books but on the top there was a battered envelope folder which had the words *Rebecca Andrews Papers*. Kate took it out and lifted back the flap. It had a passport and a degree certificate. There were also some birthday cards.

Kate looked round at the door, keenly aware that she was prying. She could hear Jimmy's voice from the kitchen, probably talking to Col who had finished his shower. She opened the birthday cards. *To Becky, all my love, Jimmy. To Becky, I love you, Jimmy. To Becks, best friends always, Jimmy.* Three birthdays.

Jimmy and his girlfriend had been together for a long time. Kate put them back. She wondered what Becky was like. She lifted out the passport and opened it at the back. Rebecca Andrews stared back at her. Kate was surprised to see that Becky looked a little like her (or perhaps it was that she looked a little like Becky). She had jaw-length dark hair and pale skin. The photo was tiny but there was something alike about her and Becky. Becky had a serious look on her face. Becky had a fringe and Kate didn't but apart from that they were similar.

"Kate, food's ready," Jimmy called.

She put the passport and the cards back into the folder and closed the box. Did she mind looking like Becky? Did it matter that Jimmy might have been attracted to her because he was pining for his ex-girlfriend?

Kate went back into the kitchen.

"Five-star noodles," he said, holding his hand out with a flourish.

Col was standing with a towel around his waist. His hair was wet and he was carrying the clothes he'd been wearing over his arm.

"See you guys," he said.

He shuffled away and Kate saw an opened bottle of wine on the table and, in the middle, a single candle that Jimmy had lit.

"I'm hungry," she said and picked up a fork and started eating.

Later, after they finished the wine, he walked her back to her house. It was noticeably chillier than earlier and she hugged herself as she walked along. He talked about his course and his plans to become a college lecturer. His words were mildly slurred and she was feeling a little drunk herself.

At her front door he seemed embarrassed. She wondered

if he was going to kiss her. Hadn't they slept together acouple of nights before? Hadn't he undressed her?

"Anyway, I'll give you a call," he said and turned to go.

"Wait," she said.

She grabbed his bare arm, a little colder now, and pulled him towards her.

"You could stay tonight," she said.

"Only if... If that's OK. I don't want to seem pushy..."

She stared at him in the dark of the porch. He'd had the same girlfriend for three years and he didn't know how to *be* with a new girl. She went on tiptoes and angled her face up to his and kissed him on the mouth. She slipped her hands under his arms and round his back. His muscles were tense and hard. She touched his lips with her tongue and felt his shoulders soften as he leaned into her.

"Let's go up to my room," she whispered, taking his hand.

He followed her into the house.

TEN

Kate woke early. When she opened her eyes she could see the light poking in around the edge of her blind. Beside her, sleeping soundly, was Jimmy. He had his back to her and the sheet was pulled up to his chin. The clock showed 05:58. She sat up, carefully, trying not to wake him. It was cold. She edged the blind back and saw the grey morning outside. There were spits of rain on her window.

The weather had broken. It didn't surprise her.

She got dressed, pulling on socks and trainers for the first time in weeks. She put on a T-shirt and grabbed her hooded top. She picked her phone up off the bedside table and noticed the condom packet. The cellophane had been pulled off, the packet open, the remaining condoms spilling out. She looked at the sleeping figure and wondered whether she had made a good choice. She thought about waking him up but decided not to. She picked up a piece of paper and scribbled a note.

Had to go out. Help yourself to breakfast (my cupboard). I'll ring you. Kate.

Downstairs she went to the fridge and got out a bottle of water and drank half of it down. Would she ring him? Or just wait until she bumped into him again.

She picked up her keys and left.

The streets were empty and she headed for the esplanade. She zipped up her top and put the hood up. Pushing her hands into her pockets, she walked down onto the empty beach. The tide was partly out and in front of her was an expanse of flat packed sand, like wet cement.

It wasn't the first time she'd gone for an early morning walk along the seafront. Usually it exhilarated her. The grey sky and the sea breeze and even the rain didn't bother her. Just being there was enough to energise her, make her feel alive. Today though, the further she walked, the more disturbed she felt. She realised that the previous evening with Jimmy had indeed only been a distraction. The events of the previous afternoon crowded in again and hung heavily over her.

She thought about the Mills family who had been staying in one of the holiday centres in Sandy Bay. The older brother had gone partying on the beach with other teenagers and somehow his nine-year-old sister had gone along. That was why people thought she had drowned. It made sense. A party on the beach; what young girl could have resisted a paddle in the sea at night?

But none of this had anything to do with her, she thought, a feeling of frustration building up inside her chest. She was in the wrong place at the wrong time, like dozens of other people. But none of those people had her background, her history.

After a while she reached the area of the beach where the cliff jutted out and the coastal path went inland. She stood for a minute feeling quite puffed. She looked up at the promontory where she'd sat on Friday evening, drinking red wine from a plastic beaker and thinking about her life. She'd thought about the letter she had written. She'd weighed up her decision to break the rules and contact Lucy Bussell. She'd even thought, for a few fearful moments, about whether it was possible that she might be sent back to prison. A women's prison.

Now that fear seemed like a joke. Now she appeared to be in *real* trouble. Not because she was guilty of anything but because of who she was and what she'd done eight years before.

It was raining properly. She put her hands in the pocket of her sweatshirt and walked off the beach past a boarded-up café and through an empty car park. She looked at her mobile. It showed 06:44. It was Tuesday morning – the holidaymakers had yet to wake up. She headed for the coastal path, following the yellow arrow that pointed to a path on the right.

She paused when she noticed two police cars parked in a layby further along.

She turned onto the path. About twenty steps further on she saw that the walkway ahead had been closed off. Police tape had been zigzagged from a fence post to a gnarled and twisted tree to stop people going any further. She went up to the tape. About ten metres ahead she saw a white tent in a field to the left. The tent was in the far corner – a sort of inflatable structure, with people going in and out of it wearing white boiler suits. One of them was holding an umbrella up and talking to one of the others.

It was the place where the girl's body had been found.

"Fancy seeing you," a voice came from behind.

She turned round.

It was DC Simon Kelsey. She looked at him with dismay. He was grinning at her. He was wearing a suit, shirt and tie and his hair had the same little sticking-up spikes in the front. The rain was falling on him but he didn't seem bothered.

"What you doing here?"

"Nothing. I just…"

"They say killers always return to the scene of the crime."

"Don't be ridiculous…"

There was no one else around. The people working around the tent were too far away to hear anything and the path behind DC Kelsey was empty.

"I just came out for a walk… I couldn't sleep…" she stuttered.

"Bad conscience?"

"No! I just felt…"

She shook her head angrily and took a step towards him to the side, to pass him, to get away from him. He stepped backwards, blocking her way.

"Excuse me," she said.

He shook his head.

"It doesn't surprise me that you're interested in our crime scene. See it, over there? We always erect a covering of some sort to keep prying eyes away, to keep the scene of crime intact. That way we can make sure that any evidence is collected. I'm forgetting though. You're no stranger to a crime scene. You've been at one yourself. Tell me, Jennifer, what was it like?"

"Stop it," she said.

She stepped the other way, trying to edge past him, but he stood fast against her and she felt the knots from the trunk of the tree sticking into her back.

"When you hit her, Jennifer, what did it feel like? To have *a person's life* in your hands?"

"Leave me alone!"

"Would you like to see this crime scene? They'll be gone soon and I can arrange to show it to you. I can point to the place where the body was," he said, his voice dropping to a whisper.

"Get out of my way!"

"I was one of the first people on the scene. She was under some bushes and covered with loose leaves and branches. All pretty rudimentary, as if done in a hurry. Not unlike your history, Jennifer. You tried to bury someone, didn't you? Not very well, as I understood it. I've read about it, see? I'm that kind of policeman. I do my homework."

She was on the brink of crying. Her throat was bursting with anger and she roughly pushed him away with both hands. He stumbled back, taken by surprise. She brushed past him, running down the steps, tearing along the path until she came out onto the road. A car passed by, its windscreen wipers swinging back and forth. She went through the car park, her jaw trembling, her eyes misting. She strode out across the hard wet sand and headed for the very edge of the sea. The tide was trickling in, the water barely deep enough to edge up the side of her trainers. She looked back up towards the café and the car park.

He was there, standing watching her.

She turned to face the sea. It was pitted with rain.

What if she were to walk into the sea and not come back? If she let the salt water claim her, take her away? She pictured herself under the surface, the silence sucking her down, her mouth open, her eyes seeing emerald green before everything went black.

She wasn't brave enough to do that though.

When she turned back to the shore DC Kelsey had gone.

She trudged along the beach in the direction of her house. It took longer going back, the wind and rain in her face. She was soaked by the time she got there and was relieved to see that everyone was out. Sally and Ruth had gone to work and Jimmy had left.

She sat on her bed. She knew she couldn't go to work. She sent a text to Aimee saying she was ill. Then she got undressed, pulled the duvet up round her head and closed her eyes.

ELEVEN

She had to go to work on Wednesday because it was Aimee's morning off and she was in charge. There was an older woman with her, Grace, a volunteer part-time worker. Grace was talking to some young people about boat trips, showing them leaflets and explaining how to book tickets. Kate left her to it and got back onto the computer to finish some paperwork.

She was updating the details on accommodation at bed and breakfast establishments. There were a number of old businesses but she'd also noticed a whole raft of homeowners offering just one double room en suite. She made a note to contact other tourist information centres to see if they had the same thing happening in their area. It might be possible, she thought, to develop a whole new page for the website offering this type of accommodation.

She was glad to be busy. After she'd finished she made some coffee for her and Grace. While she was drinking it her eye settled on one of the vintage seaside posters that they had on the wall of the shop. It was a cartoon drawing of a family walking energetically along the esplanade. The adults had formal clothes on, the man wearing a suit and a hat. The boy was wearing short trousers and a cap but the girl was wearing a dress, tied up at the back with a bow. Creeping behind them was a pickpocket and the slogan was *Keep Your Valuables Safe!*

Kate thought of the families who trudged in and out of the tourist information office trying to finds ways to keep their children entertained. They saw hundreds every week. Since she'd worked here she'd probably spoken to more than a thousand parents who all asked similar questions. *Is there anything for the children to do? Are there child-friendly attractions? What can we do with the kids?* The parents were often nice but some were irate, annoyed; spending two weeks in close contact with their children was often not the relaxing experience they thought it would be.

And the children themselves were sometimes badly behaved.

"Aimee bought Louise a lovely frock, yesterday," Grace said. "Broderie anglaise. Absolutely beautiful and cost a bit, but you know Aimee. Nothing's too good for that little girl."

Kate murmured agreement and then, in that moment, she remembered how the teddy bear badge had ended up in Jodie Mills' pocket. She almost cried out.

It had happened on the previous Thursday, the day before the girl went missing.

The family had come into the shop about four o'clock. Kate noticed the time because she was starting to think about leaving work at five and was glancing at the clock. The mother was pushing a young child in a buggy and the father had a toddler in his arms. An older girl, who looked about ten, seemed apart from them, and was on the other side of the shop, flicking through leaflets, taking fliers out of the stacks, looking at them and and then discarding them haphazardly. Every now and again the mother called across *Don't, Jode!* but the girl just continued. Kate was filling in some paperwork and only glancing at her from time to time. She did notice a teenage boy outside the door standing waiting. Kate briefly wondered if he was with the family but mostly she just tried to concentrate on the spreadsheet she was filling in. Then the girl started to sing, a recent pop song that Kate knew, and she kept repeating the same two lines over and over. Even Aimee stopped talking to look over at the girl.

The toddler got down from his father's arms and came over to Kate. He pointed at the badge she was wearing, shaped like a teddy bear. He liked it. He was sweet and was chatting nonsensically at her, pointing at the bear's face on her badge.

She gave it to him. He ran off to his dad and started a nonsense conversation with him. Kate looked away. It was twenty past four and as it was quiet she thought she might be able to leave work early. The older girl moved across her field of vision and then there was the sound of the toddler crying. Kate glanced over. The girl had Kate's badge in her hand. The girl made eye contact with Kate as if to challenge her to say something but then the door of the shop opened and a group of elderly people came in. Kate groaned. She wouldn't get away before five after all.

"You all right?" Grace said. "You look a bit distracted."

"I'm fine," Kate said shakily. "I've just got to make a call."

She went into the staff area at the back of the shop and called

Julia. When her probation officer answered she poured out what had happened and asked her to arrange another interview with DI Heart. Julia agreed, sounding pleased and positive and Kate ended the call smiling, feeling a sense of relief.

The interview couldn't take place until the early evening. Kate took the bus to Exeter because Julia couldn't make it. She didn't mind that Julia wasn't there. She just wanted to get it over and done with. She was shown straight into the same interview room that she'd been in days before. After a few moments DI Heart came in and gave the smallest of smiles. The detective pulled out a chair and sat down. She looked pale, her face drained of colour, no make-up, her hair pulled back. She was wearing a grey shirt and dark trousers. The only decoration she had on was the garnet ring.

There was no one else in the room and no recording equipment. Kate told her story. DI Heart had a pad in front of her and took some notes. When Kate had finished she closed the pad and looked straight at her.

"Odd that you didn't remember this before, Kate."

"It was such a small incident. It only took seconds and I never registered it. It wasn't until I was at work that I remembered it."

"But didn't you think about the girl after she went missing? You didn't link *this girl* to the missing girl?"

"No, we see lots of children with their parents, every day."

DI Heart nodded. "Well, it is interesting that you should come in today, because I was going to telephone your probation officer in the morning and tell her that we wouldn't need to speak to you again regarding this investigation."

"Why?"

"Because we are following other lines of enquiry."

"You've found out who killed Jodie?"

"We are investigating a number of possibilities," DI Heart said, with a forced smile.

A feeling of relief hit Kate. It was over. She would not have to come to the police station again.

"But you know who did it? And now you know that I had nothing to do with it?"

"I can't say any more than I've said."

Kate frowned. DI Heart's face had a closed look. She was using her words frugally. Kate was suddenly annoyed. After what she had gone through DI Heart *owed* her something. She spoke in a loud whisper.

"You pulled me in just because of my history."

"Not quite. You were in the area on the night it happened." DI Heart leaned forward, her elbows on the table.

"There were a lot of people at Sandy Bay on Friday."

Kate remembered coming down from her spot at the top of the cliff and passing people from the campsites, most of them still in swimming costumes and flip flops even though it was almost dark.

"There was the badge in the girl's pocket. We had to ask."

"You jumped to conclusions," Kate said, sulkily.

"Of course we did. That's what we're paid to do. We are investigating something. If leads come up we have to follow them. You can go now."

DI Heart stood up.

"That's it? My life's been miserable for days and that's it! No apology?"

DI Heart looked surprised. Kate thought for a horrible moment that she might *laugh*.

"You expect an apology, Kate? You expect a police officer to say sorry to *you*?"

"I meant…"

Why had she said that! What on earth had made her say that!

"Kate," DI Heart said, her tone pleasant but firm, "was it not made clear to you, when you were released, that this is your life now? Wherever you go, no matter what you do, you are on the database of the local police force and if it is deemed that you need to answer questions about something then you will be brought in. That's the price you pay for living freely. That's the price we, as police officers, charge, for allowing you to live among us. We know where you are, where you work, what you are doing and if you come onto our radar we will make ourselves known to you."

Kate glanced at the door. DI Heart's voice had risen. She did not want anyone else to hear; DI Simon Kelsey for example.

"You killed someone, Kate. You took their life away. Did you think six years in a restricted unit was the sum total of your punishment?"

"No, I…"

DI Heart was fiddling with her ring. She was shifting the big stone from side to side. Kate could see that it was loose on her finger.

"The dead girl, what was her name? *Michelle Livingstone*. She would be your age now. Do you ever think about that?"

"I do. Of course I do…"

"She would be at university. Or she might be working. She might have a partner or be intending to marry, have a family. Her parents would have had all that to look forward to but none of that will happen. You did that, Kate. Whatever set of mitigating circumstances your barrister offered, it was still you who took that girl's life away. Nobody else."

"You don't have to tell me that…" Kate said, blinking back tears.

"So don't ask me to apologise. Never ask me to apologise to you!" DI Heart said, her face pink, a slight quaver to her voice.

DI Heart walked over to the door and held it open. Kate went past her and scurried along the corridor. She'd come this way before; she knew her way out. She heard someone from behind call the officer's name and heard her stop and talk. Kate walked on and burst out of the exit door into the car park. She stood very still feeling the warmth of the early-evening air after the chill of the air conditioning inside the station.

As she walked back to the bus terminal she cringed at the things DI Heart had said to her. No, she didn't think of what Michelle Livingstone's life would have been like. Not because she didn't care. Not because she was trying to forget what had happened. She would *never* forget that day. She could not bear to picture Michelle at university, getting married, having babies, becoming a doctor or a teacher or even a policewoman. If she ever allowed herself to think of Michelle, it was as a ten-year-old girl. For Kate Michelle would always stay that age and as she grew older, as her life went on, she would forever turn a corner or glimpse a child crossing a road and see the ghost of the girl she killed. Eternally ten years old.

The bus came and she got on it.

Now she was feeling angry. Why did DI Heart think she could speak to her like that when she'd done *nothing wrong!*

This is your life now! the policewoman had said.

She'd been Kate Rickman for two years. She'd taken the identity they had given her and tried to live a decent life. But at any moment someone might find out who she was and then she would pack everything up, like she did before, move on, start again, somewhere else. When people realised who they'd been working with, living with, *being* with they would be shocked. *She seemed so normal*, they might say. *Who'd have guessed? You don't expect that kind of thing to happen here, in Exmouth.*

Kate thought suddenly of the detestable DC Simon Kelsey. What was to stop him dropping a hint to a journalist? Then she would wait day by day for a phone call from Julia Masters to tell her that her new identity had been exposed.

She would start over again. They would choose somewhere new for her, inform her of her new name and give her yet another fictional background. All lies.

She didn't want that. She wanted to be in control of her own life – but she kept being told she'd given up that right. Was she always to be some kind of puppet, her strings pulled by the authorities? *We've freed her*, they might say. *We've rehabilitated her. We've allowed her to resume her life!* But all the while they controlled what she could do. Would she have ever paid enough?

She got off the bus and strode along, her indignation propelling her along the street. She turned into her road and found that she was talking in a low voice, under her breath. She was upset. Now she was talking to herself? Was she going a little bit mad? She was already taking antidepressants. What else would she have to take to cope with this life of hers? Scrabbling about in her bag she pulled out her front door keys and opened the door.

The house was quiet. She was alone. She sat on the bottom stair.

What if she were to leave? Get on a train out of Exmouth. Buy a one-way ticket for somewhere of her own choosing? Decide on a new name for herself?

That would finally be an identity that no one could take from her.

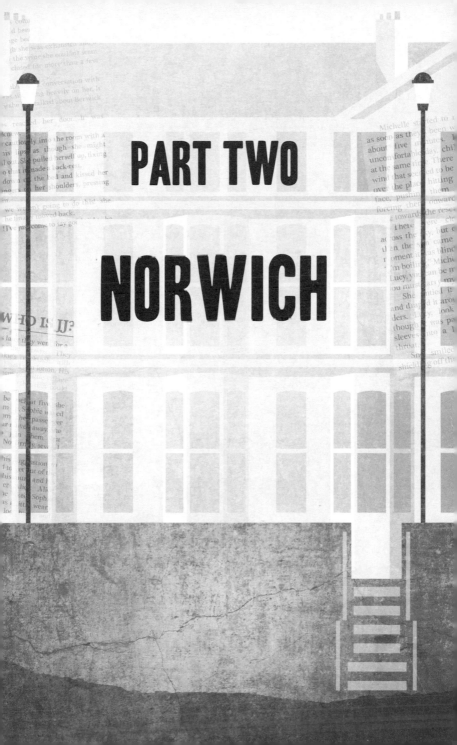

PART TWO

NORWICH

TWELVE

Jennifer Jones stood looking down at the dead girl on the ground.

She was shaking uncontrollably. Through her tears she could see that her hands were filthy. She'd been scrabbling in the dirt searching around at the place where she'd thought Michelle would be. There were welts on her skin where the branches had scratched her, where roots had jabbed her, where stones had grazed her. From time to time she'd looked intently into the bushes expecting to see the thin, still face of a cat staring at her. Still though she dug, flinging the dirt around, unable to believe that the hole was empty.

Hadn't it been just twenty-four hours earlier that she had placed Michelle there, covered her in branches? Made a kind of grave for her?

And hadn't she been watched by the creature when she did it?

Michelle had moved; metres away. How was that possible?

A policeman was standing on one side and a park ranger on the other. They were surrounded by trees and bushes which cut out the light. It seemed like night-time even though it was the middle of the day. Behind them Lucy Bussell was standing silently.

Michelle was lying on her front, her face staring into the ground. The back of her pink jumper was grimy. Her muddy trainer looked twisted, the other still white. Her red hair still sprang out from her head. She might have been sleeping.

"Don't let the children see this," the policeman had said but it was too late. Jennifer had seen it and so had Lucy.

The ranger was dumb. He was still holding his first aid box. Jennifer wanted to say something, felt she ought to explain in some way. The policeman looked a bit sick. He turned away and began talking rapidly into his radio. Jennifer couldn't catch the words but the tone was clear; panic. The ranger came across to her and put his hand on her shoulder.

"Did you see what happened?" he said to her, gently. Then he called across her shoulder at Lucy Bussell, "Did you?"

Lucy must have shaken her head, her voice disappearing down her throat.

"Who could have done this?" the ranger said.

At that moment a terrible blackness seemed to come over Jennifer, a sense of falling into a deep dark hole. She looked around for something to lean on but nothing was close and her feet wouldn't move.

The ranger put the first aid box down on the ground. Jennifer stared at it. It was white with a red cross on it and looked like a child's toy. Inside there would be plastic scissors and make-believe medicine. For a second she thought of Macy, her old doll, in her room back at the cottage; Macy, whose best days had gone, whose hair was thin and whose limbs didn't move quite so smoothly now.

The policeman's voice cut across her. He was speaking partly to someone on the other end of the line and partly to the ranger.

"I need scene-of-crime officers and detectives. For God's sake get the parents out of the car park. You, my man, take the girls back, away from here. This is a crime scene. Get them back to the Land Rover. Some other officers will be along."

The ranger looked around the space.

"I've got a daughter of my own…" he whispered.

"For God's sake, man!" the policeman shouted. "Get those children back to the Land Rover. Get them away from here. And on no account are the parents to come here. Do you understand?"

The ranger nodded and went to take Jennifer's hand. She flinched and he looked down at her palm and then at the other one.

"Your skin is scratched. What have you done to your hands? I'll have to bathe them."

He picked up the first aid box and with his free hand took Lucy's and walked on.

"Come on, dear. We'll get that looked at."

They walked through the trees and emerged onto the rough path that was prohibited to the general public. Lucy had found her voice and was talking, explaining about her brothers' den and how they'd come up to the park the day before to have a look at it and how Michelle had been in a bad temper. The ranger kept looking round at Jennifer, a frown on his face, his eyes flicking down at her hands.

Lucy carried on describing how she had *fallen* into the water.

Jennifer looked at the small girl with gratitude. She wasn't saying that Jennifer had pushed her in. She was, even now, trying to keep Jennifer out of trouble. But after Jennifer pushed Lucy into the lake she had done a dreadful thing. The memory of it made her legs buckle under her and she didn't feel she could walk another step.

"Wait…" she said, stopping Lucy's flow of conversation.

The ranger looked at her with concern.

"I don't feel well," she said.

"Of course you don't," he said, letting go of Lucy's hand and putting his arm around her shoulder. He smelled of tobacco and dirt and for a second she put her head against his shirt. He went on talking in a low voice. "You've just seen a terrible thing. The worst thing ever. When we get back to the car I'll bathe your hands and then we'll get you back home to your mum. We've got to get the police here and find the person who did this."

She could have said something then but she didn't want to upset him, disappoint him. She wanted him to have a good opinion of her, even if it was only for a short while.

She sat in the back of the Land Rover as it negotiated its way slowly along the tracks, twisting and turning, rising over hillocks and back down again. She had her palms flat out in front of her. The dirt was cleaned off and they were pink but stinging. *You might need a tetanus*, the ranger had mumbled, using antiseptic wet wipes to clean the dirt away.

Lucy was beside her but there was a huge gap between them. Jennifer put her face up against the window. The sun seemed to flash on and off, pushing its way out between clouds.

It dazzled on the lake for seconds, then it vanished and the water became brown and sloppy again.

The car park was up ahead. When they'd left it, Michelle's parents, Mr and Mrs Livingstone, had been there with a female officer. They'd been in their own car and had wanted to go with them into the park to find Michelle. They'd been told to wait with the policewoman. There'd been an argument but the policewoman had been firm. Jennifer had stared at Mrs Livingstone as they'd driven away. Mrs Livingstone's eyes had looked a little mad, shifting this way and that, and she'd been chewing her lip. Her hair, which was usually so nicely curled, stuck out and was lopsided; as if she'd been sleeping on one side of it for days and days. Mr Livingstone just looked angry and was still arguing with the officer as they drove away, pointing into the air with a finger.

Now Jennifer had to face them again. She crossed her arms and sat with great trepidation as the Land Rover turned back into the car park.

People were milling round, talking on phones. The Land Rover moved slowly round and parked on the far side.

"I want you both to stay here while I speak to these officers," the ranger said.

He got out and walked quickly across the car park. Mrs Livingstone saw them and perked up, tugging her husband's arm. The sight of her made Jennifer feel woozy. She didn't think she could speak to Mrs Livingstone ever again. She sank down in the seat. The ranger walked across to the female police officer. He had his back to Mrs and Mrs Livingstone. Jennifer's eyes were just above the line of the window and she saw Mrs Livingstone's face take on a determined expression. The woman took a couple of steps and then broke into a half run. Her husband called after her and the policewoman and the ranger turned and saw her go.

Mrs Livingstone wrenched the door of the Land Rover open. A blast of cold air hit Jennifer and she began to shiver.

"Jennifer. Why didn't you tell me that Michelle was up here, yesterday? That she was injured, hurt? Why did you lie? You could have just said. Because of you my Michelle lay out in the cold all night long. How could you do that? Jennifer, answer me! Tell me why you didn't tell your mother or me! Why did you make up a story?"

"I…" She couldn't speak, didn't know what to say, didn't know how to say it. All she could do was stare at Mrs Livingstone.

The policewoman had come up and put one hand on Mrs Livingstone's arm. She had a pained expression on her face. Behind her, where the other cars were parked, Jennifer could see the ranger talking to Mr Livingstone. He had a hand on Mr Livingstone's shoulder and his mouth was close to his ear. He was shaking his head, his lips opening and closing.

"Don't pull me away." Mrs Livingstone's voice was loud, scratchy, as if her words were rubbing against sandpaper. "I want this little tearaway to know! I want her to know that this isn't the end of it. I'll contact social services. There's no control in the family. None at all. The mother couldn't care less. She's too busy servicing men to care what this young lady does. I'll see that she doesn't come back to school. I'll complain to the council and get her mother moved on…"

"Mrs Livingstone," the policewoman said, taking her more

firmly, pulling her arm so that she let go of the door of the Land Rover. "Girls, get in the back of that police car by the entrance," she added.

They got out. Jennifer watched as Mrs Livingstone walked back towards her husband. He was leaning on the roof of the car, his forehead on his hands. The ranger was patting him on the back. Lucy got to the car first and then Jennifer got in.

"Put your seat belts on, girls," the driver said.

The car door shut and Jennifer looked over to where Mr and Mrs Livingstone were. The female officer was talking to them and Michelle's mother had both her hands up, covering her face. All of the officers nearby had stopped what they were doing and were staring at the couple.

Mrs Livingstone's legs seemed to give way and she fell forward onto the tarmac. A flurry of police officers stepped forward to pick her up just as their car turned and made its way out of the car park. It swept out onto the country lane and after a few moments drove along past the row of cottages on Water Lane. Jennifer's eyes clung to them, singling out her front door. Perhaps her mum was inside, in her bedroom, getting ready to go out. Her mum was always somewhere else when a drama was going on. Like the time when Lucy's mum had had a heart attack, she'd just slept through it. No doubt she was, at that very moment, standing in front of her mirror, deciding whether to wash and blow-dry her hair again.

Jennifer closed her eyes.

Her mother was always busy when Jennifer needed her.

THIRTEEN

At the police station Lucy went off with the policewoman who had driven them there and Jennifer was passed on to another officer who said her name was *Margaret*. She hurried Jennifer into a room with a sofa and armchairs and a low coffee table. Jennifer sat on the sofa and Margaret gave her a drink of squash and a cellophane packet of digestives. There was light green carpet on the floor. It seemed unreal and strange that she should be there in that comfortable room while everyone else was still up at Berwick Waters. She pulled at the corner of the cellophane and nibbled a biscuit. It crumbled on her tongue but she had trouble swallowing. She put the packet down and drank the squash. She wondered what was happening by the lake. She pictured a line of policemen walking along the winding path up towards the place where Michelle was. Maybe two of them would be carrying a stretcher.

Margaret was talking but Jennifer couldn't really latch on to what she was saying. She was thinking of Mrs Livingstone, in the car park. Her angry words were still ringing in Jennifer's ears. A knock on the door startled her. Margaret stood up promptly and went across to open it. It was Jennifer's mother, Carol Jones.

"Jen, there you are! I've been waiting for ages. What's going on? They said you showed them where Michelle was…"

Her mother had made an effort with her appearance but she didn't look like her usual self. She had no eye make-up on and wasn't wearing any of her fashionable clothes. Her hair was pulled up on top and she was wearing a blouse and a skirt. There was no jewellery apart from a pair of old hoop earrings. It was the kind of outfit Mrs Livingstone might have worn when she worked as a school secretary. Her mum didn't mind dressing up for Mr Cottis, the photographer. Now she was doing it for some other reason.

"Mrs Jones, DI Temple wants me to talk to Jennifer. She'll be along shortly and you'll be present of course."

"What about?"

"Just a statement. To see if Jennifer can recall any details that might help…"

"Help what?" she said, sitting on the sofa next to Jennifer.

"Michelle's dead, Mum," Jennifer said, a catch in her voice.

"I know that," her mother said, tersely, and then, turning to Margaret, she half whispered, "Hasn't my Jen done enough?"

"I don't think it will take very long…"

"Can I have a few minutes with Jen alone? Just mother and daughter stuff."

"Sure. Would you like a tea? We have a machine."

"Yes please. Black, no sugar. Jen? You want a tea?"

Jennifer shook her head as Margaret went out of the room. As soon as the door closed her mother put her arm round her and hugged her tight. Jennifer was surprised, astonished. Her mother's bony frame squashed into her and she felt herself welling up, tears coming to her eyes. Her mother *knew* that she hadn't meant to do it. Her mother understood. She would back her up. She would be there for her. She put her arms up round her neck and felt her mother's face on her skin.

"Jen," her mother whispered, her voice barely loud enough to hear, "Don't say anything about the photos or Mr Cottis. The police won't understand. They'll make it look bad and you'll be taken into foster care. You don't want that. Just don't mention him and don't say a word about the photos. You got that?"

Jennifer felt her mother's hot breath on her ear. Had she heard her right? Had she misunderstood? She nodded anyway and held onto her even though she felt her begin to disengage, move back, pull her arm away. Then her mother was sitting along the sofa and Jennifer felt chilled where her arm had been. Now there was a gap between them; enough room for a whole other person to sit.

"I'm desperate for that cup of tea. What happened to Michelle? Did you see anything? Is that why they want you here?"

The door opened abruptly and Margaret came in carrying two paper cups. She was followed by a woman in a dark suit who had a folder full of papers in her arms.

"Good afternoon. I am Detective Inspector Ellen Temple."

She came into the room but sat on a chair that was next to a table in the corner. It was Margaret who sat opposite them, making herself comfortable, smiling at Jennifer. The DI seemed to be sorting through papers. Then she looked straight at Jennifer.

"Are you feeling all right? My officer said that you had hurt your hands."

Jennifer held her hands out. They were scratched and red. She let her eyes blur while looking at them. She was thinking of Mr Cottis and his camera and the photographs her mother didn't want her to talk about. If only she knew. Jennifer would never have told anyone about those photos. She was too ashamed.

"What's wrong with your hands, Jen?" her mother said, "How come you didn't tell me? She's a bit like that," she said to the officer. "Keeps things to herself."

Margaret spoke. She appeared to be in charge even though the DI, who was looking at a mobile phone, seemed more important. She had her shoulder to Jennifer as if she was only half listening to them talking.

"Jennifer," Margaret said, "I'll be taking this interview. The DI is here just to note down anything that she thinks is important. Today, you were able to take our officer to the spot where you'd seen Michelle, yesterday."

Jennifer nodded. She was on the edge of her seat, waiting for the *accusations*.

"We want to start at the beginning. We want you to tell us what happened when you and Lucy and Michelle went up to the reservoir yesterday."

Margaret smiled and then looked at Carol Jones. Jennifer said nothing. *They knew. They'd seen what she'd done. Why did they want her to go over it all again?*

"Don't worry, you won't get into trouble for it."

Margaret's voice was light and sweet but the DI sat in the corner looking serious. Jennifer started talking, her words croaky.

"It was Michelle's idea. We went up there to mess around with Lucy's brothers' den. We thought it was like a hut or a wooden shelter, a proper building, but it turned out to just be this tin box buried in the ground. It was full of stuff, ropes and sleeping bags and other things," she said, remembering, with dread, the baseball bat.

"And while you were on your way, Jennifer, did you pass anyone? Any adults? Any teenagers? A man, perhaps?"

She frowned and tried to think back. They had seen people, some in the distance, some walking their dogs. But they hadn't come close to anyone.

"No."

"You didn't get the sense that anyone was following you?"

"No, I don't think so."

"Don't be nervous," Margaret said. "What we're trying to do here, is build up a picture of what happened, yesterday morning. Now, we know that you and your friends went up there together but then you split up. Lucy Bussell came back on her own and left you and Michelle there. What we're trying to find out is what happened to Michelle after you left."

Jennifer frowned at her. Did she mean what happened to her *body*?

"You had a row with Michelle and she walked off."

"Yes."

Jennifer remembered it, almost in slow motion. Michelle turning her back, taking a step away. *Don't bother following me! You and me aren't friends any more!* Her voice was harsh like barbed wire but still Jennifer followed her.

"Had Michelle arranged to see anyone up at the reservoir?"

"No."

"There were a lot of things tucked away under some bushes,

100

sleeping bags, tins of food and so on. Tell us about those things," DI Temple said, turning towards her.

"They were Lucy's brothers' things."

"What happened to the box that they were in?"

"I put it in the lake. I can show you the place," Jennifer said, clearing her throat. "I can even show you where I threw the baseball bat."

"Baseball bat?" Margaret said sharply.

"Yes, it had blood on it," she said.

DI Temple was frowning.

"You threw a baseball bat away? And this bat had blood on it?"

"Yes. It's in the reeds, by the lake."

DI Temple turned her chair so that it was facing Jennifer. She pushed her papers to the side.

"You saw Michelle *after* she'd been hit?"

"Yes." Jennifer was breathing hard now. She edged closer to her mother but her mother didn't seem to be paying attention to what was being said..

"But I thought you rowed and she walked off."

"We did row and she did walk off but I followed her."

"You saw what happened to her?"

Both police officers were leaning forward.

"Did you see who hit her? Who did you see? What did you see, Jennifer?"

Jennifer understood then. *They didn't know. They thought someone else had hit Michelle.*

"Now, Jennifer," DI Temple said, "did you see someone hit Michelle?"

"I…"

"What?"

"I hit Michelle."

Jennifer turned to her mother but she was looking down at her skirt, picking at something on the fabric. She willed her mother to look up at her.

"No, Jennifer, we're not talking about the squabble you had. We're talking about something much more serious. When she walked off and you followed her, did you see a man, a ranger? A walker? A teenage boy?"

Jennifer shook her head. There were too many questions.

"I didn't see anyone."

She did see the feral cat. After she'd hit Michelle she turned round and saw it sitting on a rock. It lifted its paw and began to lick it, cleaning itself as she stood and looked down at her friend on the ground.

DI Temple sighed loudly. Margaret was frowning. Jennifer glanced at her mother who looked fed up, as if she wanted to be out of there, perhaps in her bedroom getting ready to go out somewhere.

She had to tell them what happened.

"I hit Michelle with the baseball bat and then I threw it into the reeds by the lake. It was me. I did it. There was no one else there."

There was silence in the room. Then Jennifer started to cry.

FOURTEEN

Jennifer sat in her bedroom. It was quite different to the one she had in the cottage on Water Lane. This one had a window where the glass was bubbly. It gave a lot of light but she couldn't see out. The room itself was about the same size as her one at home but the door was different. It had three thin glass panels in it which let in fingers of electric light from the corridor outside at night. There was also a spy hole. Sometimes Jennifer saw the shape of one of the people who worked there as they peered into the tiny hole. They were checking on her. Like a prison warden, but they weren't called that.

The walls of her room had pictures. Scenes from fairy tales and some children's book characters. There were books to read and some games to play. There were no toys. Jennifer was too old to play with toys. She and Michelle had made that quite clear to the other kids in their class. JJ and Michelle used to read teenage magazines and listen to music and talk about boyfriends and pop bands. They left it to the other kids to play running games.

Jennifer lay back down on the bed. A single sob escaped from her lips. She turned to the side and pulled her knees up.

It was possible to take up the smallest amount of space by lying like this. But she was cold so she dragged the corner of the duvet over and covered herself right up to the bridge of her nose. Only her eyes were above it.

It was gone nine but it wasn't dark yet. She was listening for the trains. They went past at regular intervals and the sound of them seemed to get louder as the evening wore on. In the day they were just in the background but as the noise of the building died down, as the children spent quiet time in their rooms, the trains seemed to come closer as if they were running outside her window.

She wasn't quite sure where this place was. It had been a long drive in the back of a car with Jan, one of the workers, sitting beside her. *We're going to the Facility*, she'd said. They had sped through countryside and then passed streets and streets of houses, the buildings getting bigger, more and more shops and heavier traffic. Jennifer saw a sign for *Norwich Town Centre* and wondered if that was where they were heading. They passed a huge hospital and then turned off into a road that had car showrooms and some houses. The car sat at some gates for a while as Jan spoke to someone on a mobile phone. The gates opened and the car drove in and Jan took Jennifer to the place where she was to stay until she had to see the judge again.

Tomorrow her mother was coming. It would be the first time since she'd seen the judge. That was maybe a week and a half ago. She was bringing some of Jennifer's things; her clothes and schoolbooks and Macy, her old doll. She had no intention of *playing* with Macy any more, she was too old for that. It was just that she wanted something of her own there for when the door closed at night.

The solicitor was coming as well. Jennifer had already seen her a few times. Her name was Alma Morris and she had very short grey hair like a man's. She wore a dark suit and had a very heavy-looking briefcase. The handles were worn and one looked as though it was just about to rip away from the case. The solicitor told her to call her *Alma* and said that she would be looking after Jennifer while this whole horrible process was going on.

There were noises in the hallway and a face popped round the door. It was Jan.

"Main lights are being turned down now, Jennifer. You can watch your television until nine thirty. After that, room lights out."

Jennifer didn't feel like watching television so she lay in the quiet listening to the trains. When the room lights went out she stared at the strips of light from the hallway. They were like bars.

The Facility wasn't a prison, Jan had said, but Jennifer knew that it was.

The next morning the solicitor came at ten. Jennifer was in a meeting room waiting for her. There was a pot plant on the window and the same bubble glass that was in her room. Alma was puffed as though she'd run from somewhere. She was carrying her briefcase and a bottle of water which she placed on the table. Jennifer noticed a brooch on her lapel. It was in the shape of a heart.

"Now, Jennifer," she said, giving a tiny smile. "Are you OK? Are you being treated well? Is everything all right here?"

Jennifer nodded. She had Laura, the tutor, who did some reading and Maths with her. She could play Monopoly with Jan or one of the other women if she wanted or watch television in her room. She was allowed out in the small play area as long as there was someone available to be with her. There were other teenagers there, but no one her own age to talk to. It meant that she spent long periods of time on her own, but she was used to that. At least she had been used to that before they moved to Berwick. At Berwick she had had Michelle, her best friend. She had never had a friend as good as Michelle.

"Are you all right, Jennifer? You look a bit peaky."

"I'm all right," she said, her mouth dry, her eyes heavy.

"Now, I want to go over what's going to happen when we go back to court and I have some quite grown-up questions to ask you, Jennifer. I know that you're going to try and be very sensible here…"

Jennifer nodded.

"Do you know the difference between *murder* and *manslaughter*?"

Jennifer shook her head. Her teeth were firmly clenched together and her jaw felt like stone. She couldn't have opened her mouth if she wanted to. Alma was touching her hair, pulling at the strands as if she wished it was longer.

"For a person to *murder* another person they have to have planned it in advance. Like they have to have sat down and thought about it for a while. In their head they might have thought things like *I really hate that person. I want to get rid of that person. I'm going to hurt that person.* So in their head they might have decided what they were going to do. They might, if they had a gun, say…"

106

Jennifer frowned.

"Let's imagine that a man might know where a gun is, go and get that gun and wait until the person he hated had his back to him. Then he would shoot him. And kill him. Do you understand? That is *murder*."

Jennifer didn't answer. She had a picture in her head of a man with a gun. She had no idea what that had to do with her.

"Manslaughter, on the other hand, is different. It's not so serious."

The word *slaughter* seemed to fill the room.

"What *manslaughter* means is that a person kills someone else but they did it without planning it. They didn't think of it in advance. So that man I was describing might get really upset with a person and the gun just happened to be there in front of him and he picked it up without thinking and pulled the trigger."

"Like the baseball bat?"

Alma seemed to falter, shuffling her papers. She looked down at her notes for a moment. Jennifer wondered about the heart-shaped brooch on her lapel. She wondered who had bought it for her.

"Yes, Jennifer, like the baseball bat. So what we're doing is we're going to plead innocent to a charge of murder and argue that what you did is more like manslaughter."

Jennifer could only hear the word slaughter. She imagined the judge's face hardening at her, like a slab of stone. *Slaughter*.

"Will I be able to go home? After seeing the judge again?"

Alma's mouth pursed up as if she was sucking a sweet.

"I don't think so, Jennifer. I don't think you'll be going home for a while."

That afternoon her mother came. She saw her in a different visitors' room. She had a holdall with her.

"I brought your things, Jen," she said. She was still dressing the way she had when she'd been with her in the interviews at the police station. She had on a dark blouse and knee-length skirt with some flat pumps. Her hair had been trimmed and was hanging neatly around her face, as if every hair had been stuck into place. Jennifer wondered what she'd done with her other clothes, her skin-tight jeans and high-heeled shoes. She wondered if they had been packed away in a suitcase in the wardrobe of her bedroom near to where she used to keep the pink fifty-pound notes in a cardboard box.

Her mother handed her the bag. Jennifer didn't open it.

"I shoved everything in. I've been busy, what with the move. They got me a flat in Norwich. It's a bus ride from here."

"Why did you have to move?" Jennifer said, thinking of the cottage in Water Lane where they had lived.

"Neighbour's not too happy about me being there. What with Michelle's mother next door. Not that she's there now. They're staying with relatives. She'll probably move back now I've gone."

Her mother shrugged.

"This isn't bad. What are the staff like?"

"They're nice," Jennifer said. "I saw Alma, this morning, the lady from court."

"The solicitor? Yeah she's been round to me a couple of times. What with her and the social workers. Question after question. God, it's driving me mad! Honestly, Jen. I don't know what to say to you about this. I suppose it was just an accident

108

or something! You've always had a bit of a temper. Like that day you hit that girl at school…."

Jennifer remembered the day when she hit Sonia Matthews in the music lesson. It was just after the classes had gone to Berwick Waters for the day. Sonia had been friendly with Michelle and Jennifer had been upset, more upset than she could explain. Sonia had teased her, keeping on and on and then the recorder that she had had in her hand seemed to rise up and hit out at her.

"The solicitor knows of course. There are reports at school. I tried to defend you," her mother said. "I don't want them saying that you were a bad sort. No way, I'm not having that. I know you did a *terrible* thing. I'm not saying what you did wasn't *terrible* but you were always a sweet kid, Jen. Just because of this stuff up at the lake I want you to know I don't think none the worst of you. I wish it hadn't happened, of course I do."

"I wish it hadn't happened…"

But Jennifer's mother continued speaking, talking over Jennifer.

"The solicitor keeps questioning me. Like it might be my fault. Like maybe I was always hitting you so you went out and hit someone else. That's what she's saying. But it's not true, Jen. We both know that!"

Jennifer grabbed her mother's hand. It wasn't true. Her mother never hit her. Not once. She felt her mother's soft skin and let her fingers play with her mother's nails, short, unusually with no polish. After a few moments her mother took her hand back and looked around the room. Her gaze stayed on one place and Jennifer looked round and saw a camera there on the wall.

"Thing is, Jen," her mother said, leaning forward, lowering her voice. "What I said to you, in the police station, you have remembered it, right? About the photos? About Mr Cottis. You know you mustn't say a thing about them otherwise you and me will never be able to live together again."

"Why?" Jennifer said.

"People don't understand stuff like that. They read bad things into it."

Her mother exhaled a couple of times.

"They'll try and blame me. That's what the authorities are like. Then I could go to prison and then when you come out you'll have to go to foster care. We might never see each other again!"

Jennifer felt her eyes fill up. She rubbed them with her fingers. She looked away from her mother and had a picture in her mind of the days when she was first at school and she'd look out the classroom window and see her mum standing there, head and shoulders above the other mums, her blonde hair shining out, her smile lighting up the grey playground. Sometimes she'd wear casual clothes, or maybe shorts and a vest top, showing off her long legs, her tiny breasts. She was like a film star. Now she looked completely different. Just like one of the other mums.

"Don't cry, Jen. We have to keep our wits about us here. What happened was an accident, most probably, and you won't have to stay here for very long. If we keep quiet, about the photos, then we'll be back to normal in a year or two, or three."

Her mother gave her a hug before she went. Jennifer went back to her room carrying the holdall. When she got there

110

she unpacked it piece by piece. She placed her school books on the small desk and her clothes in the drawers. When she got to the bottom of the bag she frowned. Her doll, Macy, was there but she was naked. Jennifer pulled her out. Where were her clothes? She had lots of outfits in the cardboard box where she kept her. Now she had nothing on. Her mother had forgotten her clothes.

Jennifer put her back in the bag and zipped it up.

Macy was no good without her clothes. No good at all.

FIFTEEN

On the ninth of June it was her birthday. She was eleven years old. Jan came into her room after breakfast and gave her a card. On the front there was a drawing of a puppy dog and the words *On Your Birthday!* Inside it said, *Many Happy Returns from Jan and Laura.*

"There will be no celebrations, Jennifer, we don't have parties here," Jan said, "although your mother and grandmother are coming to see you today."

Jennifer nodded. She'd known there would be no party. She hadn't expected anything at all so the card came as a surprise and she'd looked at it with a sense of guilt. She would have liked her birthday to go past without anyone noticing. She wished she'd said, *Can I ignore my birthday?* But she had no idea who to say it to or whether that statement, in itself, might have been taken as her being dramatic.

So she put the card on the table beside her bed.

She'd had a birthday party the year before when they'd lived with Perry, her mum's boyfriend before they lived in Berwick. He had spent all afternoon making her a Star Wars birthday cake and given her a tiny camera as a present. Jennifer had taken photographs of the cake and of Perry's collection of Star Wars figures. When her mum came in from work she'd rolled her eyes at the cake but she'd still smiled for a photo. Jennifer had wanted to have the film developed and had taken it out of the camera but she'd done something wrong and spoiled it so the photos had never come out.

The cake lasted a few days though.

Her mother came in the afternoon with her grandmother. They had the visitors' room to themselves.

"How are you, Jen?" her gran said.

"I'm all right."

"It seems quite nice here. I've passed this place on the bus over the years but never knew it was a prison."

"It's not a prison, Mum!" her mother said. "It's a special place…"

"It's called a *Facility*," Jennifer said.

"When I used to get the twenty-nine bus. That's when I saw it."

Her gran's fingers were tapping on the table. Jennifer looked at the *No Smoking* sign on the wall and knew that her gran was suffering. Her mum leaned down to a carrier bag and pulled out a wrapped present. It was flat and looked like a book or a game.

"Thanks," she said, pulling at the paper.

"It's from both of us," her gran said "Well, I paid for it. Your mum's promised to pay me back but I'm not holding my breath."

"I will, Thursday. When I get my benefits. I told you."

It was a jewellery-making set. Jennifer smiled at it, pleased. There were rows of coloured beads and threads. There were some clasps and pins for a brooch. There was some coloured felt and on the front of the box was a photograph of a felt brooch in the shape of a flower. She was instantly reminded of Alma's heart-shaped brooch.

"This is really nice," she said.

"Well, I thought you should have something creative," her mother said. "It's good to be able to make things. Look at all the clothes your gran makes."

Her gran smiled and looked down at the top she was wearing. She fingered the neckline as though checking for a piece of thread.

"I've always made my own clothes," she said. "I'd have made some for your mum if she'd let me. But no, my dressmaking was never good enough for Miss Carol Jones! No, she wanted clothes from Topshop."

"I did wear some of the clothes you made me!"

"Hardly ever. But that was your mum, Jennifer, always did her own thing. Never cared about hurting other people's feelings."

"Don't go on, Mum."

Her gran continued talking and Jennifer looked at her mother. She was frowning and had moved her chair back a little, further away from the table. She noticed then that her mother's hair was a lighter colour than recently and she was wearing a fitted blouse which was deep pink. She had eyeliner on and it made little flicks at the corner of her eyes. She looked nice again, not like she had when Jennifer first came to the Facility.

"In any case, Mum," her mother interrupted her gran, "I was going to tell Jen about my new job. It's in a clothes shop. A friend of Mum's told me about it."

"Oh."

114

"The shop's called Sharp Style. Georgie Miller is the boss. It's just serving in the shop but he said he might get me to model the clothes so that they could put pictures of them on the walls. It's quite good money and could keep me going until things sort themselves out…"

"That's always assuming you don't muck it up, Carol."

"She won't muck it up, will you, Mum?" Jennifer said, pressing her fingers onto the corner of the jewellery box set.

"Course not."

"And make sure that Georgie keeps his hands to himself. I know what you're like…"

"Mum!"

"I tell like I see it, don't I Jen?"

Jennifer stared at her gran, who was chewing at her nails. How long was it since she'd had a cigarette? Twenty minutes? Half an hour?

"How's the dog?" Jennifer said, suddenly.

Her gran frowned at her, a look of something dark flickering across her features. Jennifer pictured Nelson, one of her gran's dogs from years before. It was a small Jack Russell breed. It had its own special armchair and it didn't like Jennifer, showing its teeth to her and growling at her from time to time. In the end it had stopped growling forever.

Her grandmother seemed to stumble over her answer. "You mean my…my Minty? She's good as gold. I had to take her to the vet the other day for her injections. Did I tell you, Carol, that I'm going to Portugal with my friend, Maureen, from bingo? Early September?"

"What about Jen's trial?"

115

"When is it?"

"We don't know exactly. In the autumn some time."

"Probably be later than September. They've got evidence to collect and witnesses to sort out. Honestly, the trouble you've caused, Jen! And that poor little girl dead."

Jennifer felt her face heat up. She studied the jewellery set. She used her fingers to flick at the glassy beads.

"And it doesn't seem to have taken a feather out of her!"

"Don't have a go at her, Mum. She's being punished."

"Not enough. I always said you were too soft on her. I always told you that, Carol. Give her a good telling off or a few thumps from time to time."

Her gran directed these words straight at Jennifer.

"Now's not the time, Mum."

"I wasn't soft on you, Carol, and you turned out all right. Mostly. Look at all those lovely photos you've had taken. Not many mums can show off pictures of their daughter in the Littlewoods catalogue. I can though."

"We best be getting off, Jen," her mum said, standing up and leaning across the table to give Jennifer a kiss on the cheek.

Her gran walked ahead, towards the door, waving as she went. Jennifer could see her patting her bag, looking for her cigarettes and her lighter.

"See you when I can, Jen," her mum said. "Remember I'm starting work next week."

Jennifer sat with the jewellery set on her lap until Laura came into the room to take her back to her block.

"That's nice," Laura said. "You can make some pretty necklaces with that."

116

When they got back to her room Laura followed her in and sat on her chair.

"I got you this," she said, holding her hand out.

It was a wrapped present, like a slim book, and Jennifer took it, feeling embarrassed. She opened it and saw a hardback book, *A Child's First Book of Prayers.*

"I know that on your notes there is no mention of religion in your family but I thought you might like to look at these. There are some lovely illustrations and you might enjoy reading some of them. It's up to you."

"Thank you," Jennifer said.

When Laura left her she looked at the book, at the pictures and the words. In school they had said prayers but it had always been just a case of remembering the lines and looking serious as she spoke. She placed the book in one of her drawers and carried the jewellery set over to her table. In the distance she could hear a train. She wondered if her mum and her gran were on it going back home to her gran's. Or was her mum going somewhere else, to someone else's room or flat? Someone like Perry who was so good at making birthday cakes.

SIXTEEN

Jennifer thought about her mother, the model.

She'd been looking through some of her old books that had been sent from her school. She was to do exercises on how to use capital letters. Laura had told her to spend thirty minutes at it and then call her to go over it. Jennifer found a new exercise book underneath a reading diary. She looked through it and was surprised to see a photograph of her mother inside the pages.

It was a very old photograph. Her mother was wearing a swimsuit. She had wedge sandals on and a sarong around her waist. She was smiling and holding a beach ball as if she was about to throw it. Behind her was the beach and the sea. It wasn't a photograph, it was a picture that had been cut out of a catalogue or magazine. She couldn't remember which. Maybe it was Michelle who cut it out.

Michelle had loved the fact that Jennifer's mum was a model. Jennifer had been proud of it herself. She had a portfolio of her pictures and she often pulled it out of the cupboard and spent time going through it, turning each page and seeing her mum look so glamorous and well dressed. Sometimes the clothes made her look like a different person; a business woman or a movie star or a top fashion model. Most of her mother's work was for clothes catalogues but her real ambition was to model the latest fashions in glossy magazines. Jennifer had pored over pictures of her mother in dresses and formal wear and casual clothes. She'd shown these to Michelle. Her friend had been impressed. *Wow!* she'd said.

But the modelling world was a hard one, her mother said. Sometimes there was lots of work but often the photographers stopped calling her and the sessions dried up and her mother stayed at home and Jennifer watched the place gently deteriorate around her. Instead of being up bright and early, instead of spending hours in the bathroom and emerging washed and made up and smelling of perfume, her mother slept late and lay around on the sofa watching television all day.

When they moved to Water Lane things seemed to improve.

Mr Cottis came. Her mother started to get more photographic work. Mr Cottis was a freelance photographer and didn't have his own studio so he brought his equipment to her house and took photographs of her mother there. Jennifer pictured him standing in their kitchen. He was tall and thin and had no hair at all. He wore glasses that went dark in the sunlight and sometimes stayed dark for a few moments when he was inside the house. It made him look strange.

He would spend ages fiddling with a camera. He seemed to have a number of them and they sat on her kitchen table while he used bits of cloth to polish sections. His tripod leaned against the wall in the corner, making it difficult to walk easily round the small room. Sometimes, if she was getting a glass of water, she found him looking at her steadily, without blinking, as if his eye was a lens that he was setting up, waiting to take a picture of her.

Mostly the photo sessions took place in her mum's bedroom. It was easier to get the camera set up in there and simpler to move her furniture round. Sometimes the sessions took a long time.

Jennifer frowned at the memory. An uncomfortable feeling dragged at her throat. She put her mother's picture aside and looked at the exercise in the book in front of her. Capital letters for place names, days of the week, months of the year. All she had to do was copy out the sentences and put the capital letters in where they should be. They went at the beginning of a sentence, everyone knew that. She copied the words out in her neatest handwriting.

On Thursday John and Sarah went to Buckingham Palace.

Her mother had to role play in these photographs. She had to dress up. Jennifer hadn't liked the way she looked. She'd seen her in a schoolgirl outfit and there were things in her bedroom that Mr Cottis must have brought; a globe, a ruler, some books. Her mother had always had to dress up in order to be a model but before it had been smart clothes in a catalogue that lots of people could look at. The photos with Mr Cottis didn't seem like that. They seemed like the kind of photos only a few people would see. Jennifer thought of Lucy Bussell's brothers, Stevie and Joe, and the picture she had found in their den up at Berwick Waters. Jennifer had gasped to see her mother like that. Michelle had seen it too. She had called it *gross*.

Soon after that Jennifer had hit her. Not once but twice.

Jennifer shrank back away from the exercise book. She put the pen down and folded her arms across her chest. She found herself rocking, remembering the day at Berwick Waters. How long ago was it? Eight weeks? Ten weeks? She had lost track of time. Here in this room she had watched day after day slip by. Sometimes her mother came to see her, more often she did not. Alma came regularly on Fridays. The women were always around, Jan or Laura; sometimes others. She could read, go out into the play area. She had a television and there were board games to play. There were others in the Facility, she could hear them but not see them, not close up. She wondered if they were alone, like her.

She wondered if they had ever seen such photos of their own mothers.

Her mother liked Mr Cottis. He was her agent and would eventually get her better work and she might end up in magazines modelling the latest fashions. And there had been lots of money after Mr Cottis's visits. Her mother pointed out a box in the bottom of her wardrobe and Jennifer first saw the pink fifty-pound notes, quite a few. Her mother bought things and gave Jennifer money and it seemed OK for a while. But then Mr Cottis's van would pull up outside their door. He would bring his camera into their house once more and Jennifer would feel anxious, her feet refusing to stay still, as if she was in someone else's house and should get out as quickly as possible.

Jennifer unfolded her arms. It made her feel cold. She stepped across to the bed and pulled her duvet off. She put it round her shoulders and stared hard at the English textbook. *Capital letters are used for proper names; street names, names of towns and cities and countries.* She tried to focus on the exercise in front of her. In the distance she could hear a train passing and she let her mind go along with it. She imagined the engine slipping through the countryside on its way somewhere, maybe taking people on holiday or on a trip to see their family or friends.

She picked up the pen and wrote, taking her time with each word.

John Morris was going on holiday to Switzerland. He was catching a plane in London. On his suitcase were labels of places he had been; Paris, Milan, Frankfurt and Amsterdam.

Then one day Mr Cottis had wanted Jennifer to pose in a photo.

Her mother had seemed strange about it. *It's a family shot*, she'd said. *I'll be there all the time. It'll be over quickly. He's really keen. It's for a magazine article he's working on. He might want you to dress up.*

There was a bag of dressing-up clothes for her. A school uniform just like the one she had seen her mother wearing after one of the sessions. It wasn't like her school uniform. She had a sweatshirt with the name of her school on it and she wore trousers or sometimes a skirt. This school uniform was old-fashioned. She didn't like it. Not one bit. She didn't want to do it. She told her mum that.

But her mother was curt in her reply. She had to do it, otherwise Mr Cottis would find someone else to be an agent for. Jennifer was lucky, her mother seemed to imply – maybe it was the first step for Jennifer on a career just like her mother's. A modelling career. But Jennifer hadn't wanted that so she went out with Michelle and Lucy up to Berwick Waters and she stayed away from the house when Mr Cottis was supposed to come.

She avoided dressing up and staring at his camera. She saved herself.

But she killed Michelle.

Slaughter. Slaughter.

The duvet was slipping off her shoulder and she pulled at the corners to hold it in place. The door opened then and Laura came in. She had a smile on her face like she usually did and she looked down at the exercise book.

"Oh!" she said. "You haven't got very far. Do you not know about capital letters? Would you like me to explain to you?"

She shook her head. She did know about capital letters, of course she did. Laura put a hand on her shoulder and she shook it off.

"Are you all right?" Laura said, looking dismayed.

She shook her head. She threw off the duvet. She grabbed up the exercise book and began to tear at the pages, pulling the one she had written on out, letting it float to the floor then using two hands she tried to pull the book apart and tear it in half but it was too strong so she shredded the pages, tearing strip after strip off. Laura backed away as she did this. She left the room and Jennifer flung the book and the textbook into the far corner of her room and sat on the floor with her duvet round her shoulders, covering her chin.

She sat like that until she heard footsteps coming along the corridor, more than one person. They came into her room and she covered her head with the duvet.

The weeks slipped by and it was darker for longer in the morning. The afternoons got shorter as the light faded behind the bubble glass. Jennifer was allowed to watch television earlier and she was given a cassette player and tapes of music to listen to. She didn't see Alma so often. Her mother was busy at work and came every other week although she rang her more often.

The trial was due to take place in October but that changed. Then it was November but it was postponed. Jennifer saw doctors and counsellors. She spent time doing personality tests. Laura went to work with some other children so she had a new tutor, Joanne. Joanne taught her some French and Latin. She helped her make a magazine full of stories and quizzes and pictures that she drew or cut out of old glossy magazines. She showed her how to string the beads of her jewellery set so that she could make a necklace. She made a felt brooch for Alma in the shape of a sunflower. Sometimes Joanne sang songs as they worked. *Frère Jacques, Frère Jacques, Dormez-vous? Dormez-vous? Sonnez les matines! Sonnez les matines! Ding, dang, dong…*

The final date for the trial was early December, Alma told her. *It'll be out of the way for Christmas. Best for everyone.* Jennifer wondered who the *everyone* was; Mr and Mrs Livingstone? Alma? Her mother? Her?

Her mother came regularly then. In the weeks before she had to go and see the judge again she saw her twice a week. Each time she looked a little different. The make-up increased, her hair was shaped and glossy-looking, her clothes were tighter and more modern. On the last day before seeing the judge she came in skinny jeans and high boots and a short leather jacket. Alma was there talking things through with her. Alma frowned when her mother walked in.

"I hope you're not intending to wear that sort of thing in the courtroom, Miss Jones?"

"Don't worry. I know how to dress for the courtroom."

When Alma left her mother rolled her eyes. "Stuck-up cow!"

Her mother talked about her job and her flat and Georgie Miller who, it turned out, was in the middle of a divorce and was spending a lot of time with her.

"Georgie's not a bad bloke. A bit old but kind. I think you'd like him."

She began to move around in her chair, crossing her legs then uncrossing them as if she couldn't get comfortable. There was an uneasy silence. As if they'd run out of things to say.

"I haven't seen Gran for a while."

"No, she's been busy."

"Is she in Portugal?" Jennifer said, remembering the holiday she was going to go on with her friend from the bingo.

"No, no. Fact is she and I are not on speaking terms. She is such a cow! You know what she said? She said it was me who broke up Georgie's marriage. That's just not true. Georgie and his wife hadn't slept together for *eight years*. But that's your gran. She knows best. She always thinks that she's right."

Her mother's mouth had twisted up..

"She's just so critical, Jen. *You're so pathetic, Carol. You got no brains, Carol. You're such a dope!"*

Jennifer frowned. She didn't like to think of her gran being horrible to her mum.

"And she goes on about how I haven't been strict enough with you and I don't know, maybe she's right. Maybe if I had this other stuff wouldn't have happened. This *hitting* Michelle. I just don't know why you did it. I don't have a clue. What made you? I just don't understand, you're such a quiet thing. Too quiet, your gran said. You're such a *little* girl and yet you've done this…"

"I don't know, Mum, I just don't know…"

Her mother looked down at the table for a few moments. She used a finger to wipe the corner of each eye. Then her hand dropped onto the leather jacket and she stroked it.

"Georgie bought this for me. He says it makes me look like Kate Moss."

"It's nice. It suits you," Jennifer said.

"I might have some pictures taken in it."

Jennifer nodded. It would make a good shot. Her mum would look glamorous in it.

"Well, this is it, Jen," her mother said, as if pulling herself together, as if she'd just remembered she had somewhere important to be. "I don't want you to be nervous tomorrow. There's a lot of people looking out for you, including me."

Jennifer nodded, a lump in her throat.

"You're going to be all right."

Her mother leaned across and gave her a kiss on the cheek. Then she stood up and turned to go. She took a step or two but came back, looking uncertain. She sat in the seat again and peered around as if making sure no one was watching.

"Jen, whatever you do, in this trial, whatever you do don't…"

"It's all right, Mum. I won't mention the photographs."

"Promise?"

"I promise."

Jennifer watched her mother leave.

SEVENTEEN

Jennifer woke up early on the day of the trial.

It was still dark and the Facility was quiet. She could hear the trains running, their sound regular and comforting. The radiators began to click, gently, as if someone in another room was tapping quietly on the pipes. Rain was splashing against the window. She could hear it pitter-patter. She lay there for what seemed like a long while.

The light from the corridor lay in stripes on the floor of her room. As it got lighter outside the colour seemed less intense and after a while she couldn't see them clearly and it was just grey daylight slipping through the window. Then there was movement on her corridor. The sound of footsteps walking along, a distant snatch of whispered conversation. More footsteps and then some doors far away in the building shutting loudly.

People would be getting up. Breakfast would be soon. And later she would go and see the judge.

It was early December. On the wall of her room was an Advent calendar that Laura had brought in. She'd said that Jennifer might like to open up each day in the lead-up to

Christmas. She didn't have to pray, Laura said, but just enjoy the pictures. The big picture was of a Christmas tree and there were lots of little windows to open which showed other Christmassy images.

Over the last few weeks Jan had bought her some new clothes so that she would look smart when she went before the judge. They were hanging in the wardrobe. She'd come into Jennifer's room holding Marks and Spencer bags and smiling as if she had a big surprise waiting for her. She'd previously asked her what colours she liked and Jennifer had thought of Macy and the outfits she used to wear. She'd told Jan that she liked pink and yellow. When Jan took the clothes out of the carrier bags Jennifer had been surprised to see dark shades; green, purple and navy blue. There were three pairs of trousers. One pair was like school trousers and the others were like jeans with pockets at the back. There were two purple jumpers, one a lighter colour than the other, and a dark green blouse with lace on the collar.

There was underwear and new boots and shoes and an anorak. Her mother had brought clothes up for her to wear over the months she'd been there but lots of them felt too tight and the trousers were short. Jennifer had grown.

She had to look smart for the judge.

Jan had sat with her the previous evening just before lights were due to go out.

"The next couple of weeks might be very difficult," she said. "I'll be at court with you for most of the time. There might be times when you'll be upset, and if you want to talk to me about anything then I'll be happy to listen to you."

Jennifer nodded.

"There'll be lots of questions asked and there might be some angry people around. You'll have to be strong and just tell the truth. Miss Morris has told you all this, I know. But if at any time you feel you want to talk…"

Jennifer knew what Jan meant. She meant if Jennifer wanted to talk about *that day;* the day when Michelle got hit and died. *When Jennifer hit her.* She'd said something similar a number of times during the weeks and months that Jennifer had been there. It was always at quiet times and Jan had sat on the end of her bed or on the chair. Her voice had been soft and inviting and yes, once or twice, Jennifer had wanted to open her mouth and utter something that would please Jan. *Michelle and I had an argument. She said things about my mum. She said she wasn't going to be my best friend any more. She turned her back on me and I had to stop her walking away. I reached out to her but there was something in my hand.* But, no, that wasn't quite true. It made it sound as though Jennifer hadn't known what was in her hand, that she hadn't understood that she'd been hitting out. Had she? She'd been fiercely angry. Her feelings had become a whorl of rage that tore into Michelle.

How could she explain that?

Now she looked at the outfit she was due to wear today. She took the hanger down and laid it on the bed. She looked up at the bubble glass and saw that it was still wet. The morning light had a dark hue as though the sky was full of rain clouds. It would be best to wear the boots, she thought.

Then, from nowhere, she had an image of Michelle in her mind. Michelle sitting in their classroom patting the chair beside her so that Jennifer would come and sit on it. Jennifer's heart had leaped at the tender way she had done it. Michelle looked round at the other children, her face beaming in a proudly possessive way as if Jennifer was a prize she had won. *You're my best ever friend, JJ,* she had whispered. *We'll be friends forever!*

Jennifer pulled the new clothes towards her. She buried her face in the green blouse with its lace collar. Her eyes blurred but there were no tears.

Today no one would need to save a seat for her.

The courtroom looked a bit like a church, Jennifer thought. It had a lot of wood and there were pews for people to sit on. When she entered it was noisy and full of people. The court usher guided the policeman, her and Jan in. The sound of talking grew quieter as she followed him around the back of the room. Then it was completely silent and she knew without looking that every single person was watching her. The policeman stood back and Jan edged her towards the central box with glass sides. This was called the *dock* and it was where she was to sit. It had all been explained to her in advance by Alma. It was where the accused sat so that everyone involved in the trial could see them clearly. She had also been told what to expect. The court would be full of grown-ups. Some would be wearing gowns and wigs and there would be a lot of talking. *She* was not to speak at all unless someone spoke to her. She was to sit quietly next to Jan or one of the other Facility workers. If she needed to go to the toilet or speak to Alma she was to write a note and give it to Jan.

She stepped inside and saw two chairs. They were both placed on a platform that had been built with new wood. It stood out against the rest of the box. She puzzled over it but then knew why. It was so that when she sat down she could see over the wooden side of the dock. The dock had not been designed for children to sit in. No one expected a child to be accused of such a crime.

The seat felt hard and cold when Jennifer sat down. Alma had told her that once she was in the court she should look straight ahead. She did this for a few minutes as the murmurings of conversation started again, this time with a whispered sound, as though people didn't want anyone to hear what they were saying. Then she looked casually around to see where her mother was sitting. Her eyes swept the rows of faces deliberately not pausing or making eye contact with anyone, just looking for the familiar face of her mother. What would Carol Jones look like today? She had told Alma that she knew how to dress for court. Did that mean she would have a dark suit like Jan was wearing? Or a jumper and skirt? What would her hair be like? Puffed up? Or combed round her face, flat and plain?

She saw a face she knew and her eyes stopped and rested on it. It wasn't her own mother, it was Mrs Livingstone. Something squeezed at her insides as she fixed her attention on Michelle's mother. She sensed people around Mrs Livingstone noticing her looking but she couldn't pull her eyes away. Mr Livingstone was there beside his wife. He appeared just the same. Jennifer would have known him anywhere. His wife seemed to have shrunk though. She was only a fraction of the woman she had been. Her long red hair had been cut off as though someone had run a razor over her scalp. Her eyes looked huge and she stared at the front of the courtroom, her gaze unbroken by Jennifer's greedy eyes. Even though there were whispers and gasps from people around, she did not look at Jennifer, not once. Neither did Mr Livingstone (*call me Frank*).

Jan must have noticed her looking because she put her hand on Jennifer's arm and pointed towards the front of the courtroom, indicating the place where her eyes should be. Jennifer tried to stare at the empty judge's chair, wondering all the time whether Mrs Livingstone was looking at her *now*, fancying that she could feel the woman's eyes burning into her skin.

There was noise from the back of the courtroom. The doors were opening and someone was coming in at the last minute just as the proceedings were about to start. Everyone looked round. So did Jennifer.

It was her mother, saying a whispered sorry to the court ushers. She was wearing a mac and her hair was pulled back in a neat tie.

How *could* she be late?

She looked up at Jennifer and gave her a quick wave and a muted smile. The usher was pointing towards the front and her mother was fumbling with her bag and an umbrella. She took some steps towards Alma who had saved some seats for her.

But Jennifer wasn't looking at her mother any more.

Behind her was a tall thin man who was wearing black trousers and a dark jumper. Over his arm was a raincoat. His head was bald and he had rimless glasses on. He glanced up at Jennifer but had no expression on his face. Even though she was far away from him she imagined an image of herself in each of his lenses.

It was Mr Cottis. Her mother had brought him with her to see Jennifer on trial. She looked down at her lap, her hands clasping each other, tightening, squeezing the bones of her fingers. Jan leaned across her.

"Don't cry, Jennifer, the judge will be in soon," she whispered, pulling a tissue from a box that was on her lap.

But Jennifer couldn't help it. She didn't take the tissue but used the sleeve of the green blouse to wipe her eyes. Then someone knocked on a table with a hammer, startling her. A wooden door opened with a baleful creak and the judge swept into the courtroom.

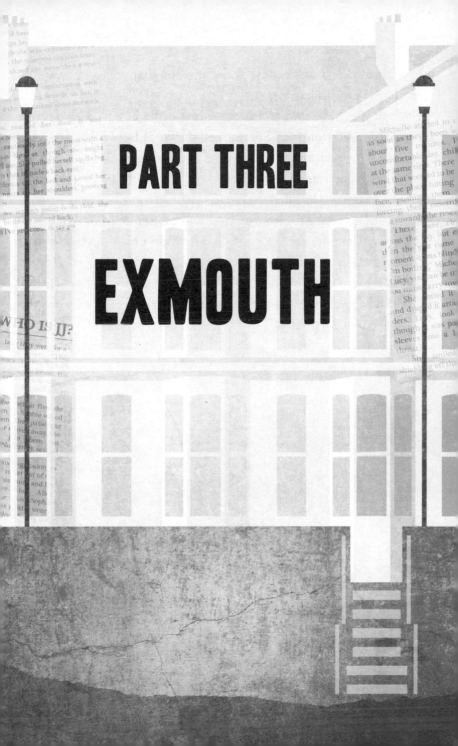

PART THREE

EXMOUTH

EIGHTEEN

A letter arrived just as Kate was leaving for work. It had a London postmark and her name and address was written in neat handwriting. She sensed it was from Lucy Bussell. She stood at the hall table and started to open it but suddenly felt odd, apprehensive. It was almost three weeks since she'd written to Lucy. Then she was firm and resolute; her motives had been clear, to make an apology of sorts. At the time she'd been brash about breaking her terms of release. It was as if she hadn't cared a jot for what the authorities might do to her. Now, after recent events, she didn't feel so confident about what she had done. Her experience with the police had unnerved her and instead of not caring whether or not she was punished she now dreaded the prospect.

Something else worried her. What if Lucy's reply was harsh? What if there were cruel words in it? She didn't think she could stand that.

She put the unopened letter into her bag and went to work.

All morning she thought about it. She wanted to slip off into the staff area and look at it in private. But work was busy and she simply didn't have the time to stop. It was her last week in the job and it had become hectic in the lead-up to the August bank holiday weekend. The influx of visitors to the town seemed to have increased and there were constant enquiries about accommodation, theatre bookings, two-for-one deals at local attractions. At times the shop seemed close to bursting. Outside, on the esplanade, work was going on in preparation for the festivities. Bunting had been strung between lampposts and the shops along the front were decorating their windows.

When it was finally quiet Aimee came across to her with the work diary in her hand.

"Kate, you're finishing this week. Last day Saturday?"

"Yes."

"I'll miss you," she said. "It'll just be me and the volunteers. Not that I don't think they're fantastic, it's just that…"

Aimee looked at the computer with consternation.

"I could show you some stuff on the computer, Aimee. It's really easy!" Kate said.

"I know. You're so sweet, Kate. And that's why I wanted to ask you a favour, about Saturday?"

"Sure."

"Could you possibly do my shift in the afternoon? I mean could we swap? I'll do the morning and you come in at one? Only I'm taking Louise to her dad's for the long weekend. He said he'd come and pick her up but I wanted to go myself and check out his living arrangements I don't want my Louise in some squat type property. I want to make sure it's clean and proper. I'll pop back in at the end of the afternoon to say goodbye."

"That's fine. I'm sure his place will be nice. He wouldn't want his daughter to stay anywhere dodgy."

"You sure it's OK? I know you said you were going camping the day *after* you finish work, so it shouldn't interfere with your plans."

"It's not a problem."

"See how I'm going to miss you! Tell you what, I'll make some tea. I've brought a packet of those pink wafer biscuits. They're my favourite, apart from chocolate…"

"And the diet?"

"After the bank holiday. Then I'll start."

Just after two Kate went out for a quick lunch. She bought a roll and some water and walked towards the beach. It was hot and the air seemed heavy. There were hardly any windbreaks on the sand and lots of people were lying by beach tents in which small children were sleeping. There was music coming from a radio somewhere, a soft female voice singing something melancholy. Kate sat on a flat rock close to the water's edge. She kicked off her shoes and let her feet rest on the hard wet sand.

Then she opened the letter.

It was three pages of lined paper closely written, torn from an A4 pad, the punched holes still there. She unfolded them, smiling to see the small neat handwriting, line after line of it. In the middle was a surprise. A small photograph sat in the fold of the paper. It had been cut from a strip of photos, the kind that gets taken for a passport or maybe an identity card in college. It showed a girl's face. On the back was written, *Lucy, 16*. Kate searched the tiny picture for some memory of the eight-year-old child that she'd known. It was impossible though. The picture showed a rather serious girl who had short spiky hair and who wore heavy earrings and dark lipstick. There was no resemblance at all to Lucy's younger self.

She read the letter, her roll and bottle of water untouched. The tone of the first few lines pushed the worries of the morning away.

Dear Kate (for security reasons I'll call you Kate). Thank you for your letter. I was on holiday when it arrived, so that's why it's taken a long time to reply. I was surprised to get it (but was not alarmed as you thought I might be). You asked what my life is like now. My mother, my brother Stevie and I are living in Wood Green, North London. Stevie is going to get married in October and I am going to be a bridesmaid. He is only staying with us while he and Terri (his girlfriend) decorate the flat they're renting. Mum and I are waiting for a housing association flat, a kind of sheltered accommodation. Mum's health isn't great (you probably remember). I've just finished my GCSEs and am waiting for my results (any day now). Then I'm going to do A levels at the local sixth form college. Stevie says it's a waste of time going to college but I usually totally IGNORE him. So that's my family situation.

I had a boyfriend for two years but we split up recently. We're still friends and I don't have anyone else yet. He's seeing this girl in year eleven (although there is gossip about her, but it's up to him, it's his choice). His name is Donny and I miss him sometimes but it is definitely over now.

*Thank you for saying sorry about what happened
at Berwick Waters. I haven't forgotten that day but it's
not on my mind a lot. The truth is I hardly ever think
about it. When something comes up in the newspaper
or it's mentioned then I do remember. But I don't
get upset about it. It was terrible (what happened to
Michelle) but I don't think you meant that to happen
so I don't blame you (whatever the newspapers said).
I feel very sad for Michelle's mum and dad. That goes
without saying.*

*The newspapers said I was a witness but I wasn't.
That night was unreal. Michelle didn't come back and
Michelle's mum couldn't stop crying. I even saw her dad
wiping his eyes with the corner of a tea towel. When I
told her mum that we'd been up at Berwick Waters it
seemed as though I'd lit a firework and it was fizzing
waiting to go off. When you went off with them up to
the lake I was expecting to see you come back (and
hear what had happened). But later that day social
services came and I was taken to foster carers. I spent
months with them (Susie and Mike Robertson, they
were really nice). The absolute truth is that I didn't
even KNOW what had happened up at the lake until
a long time afterwards when my brother Stevie told me.
I found it hard to understand. I just couldn't believe it,
it was like a story or something. Then Mum came out of
convalescence and she and me got a flat in Chelmsford
and I guess it just slipped out of my head. Stevie and
Joe lived with us for a while. We've moved around a*

bit since then (stuff happened) but I think we've settled in Wood Green now and I've got a lot of friends (and that's one reason why I'm not really worried about Donny and this new girl). I am nervous about going to the college though. Stevie says I can change my mind up to the last minute and that Terri will get me a job in her hairdressers, but I don't think I will.

So you don't need to say sorry. I always knew that whatever happened, you would be sorry. You were that kind of girl, mostly nice and friendly.

If you're ever in London call by and see me (London's HUGE. You'd need to get a map but I'm about ten minutes' walk from Wood Green tube station). My mobile number is at the bottom of this letter.

Lucy Alexander (Bussell)

Kate read it over again and glanced from time to time at the tiny photograph as if she might imagine this girl speaking to her. Then she sat back. Lucy Bussell's words made her feel heady. *I don't think you meant that to happen.* Other people had said similar things to her over the years; Jill Newton and Rosie. They had known that she hadn't meant it to happen.

But Lucy had been there on that day. Her words carried more weight.

Now she lived in London with her mother.

Almost eight million people lived in London. Kate had looked it up on the internet the night before. When she stayed in halls in her first year at university there had been a number

142

of girls from London. They talked about what it was like to live there, the traffic, the noise, the closely packed housing. It was an all-night city, they said. The pubs and clubs were open late and there were night buses and the sounds of horns or sirens into the early hours. Kate recognised this. Living in Croydon for nearly nine months had given her a taste of the big city, even if it had been on the outskirts.

She folded the letter up and put it in her bag and began to eat her roll, which had got hot sitting in the sun.

"Hi!"

She looked up. It was Jimmy. He was smiling down at her.

"Hello!" she said.

He sat down beside her, nudging up so that she had to move along on the rock. Then he put his arm around her shoulder and gave her a kiss on the side of her face. She pretended not to notice and stared at his bare feet on the sand.

"Where are your shoes?"

"In my bag. I like walking along the beach with no shoes on."

He was wearing cut-off jeans and a vest. He smelled of salt as if he'd been in the sea already that day. His skin was the colour of honey.

"The sun's bad for you," she said, taking his arm from around her shoulder and holding his hand between hers.

"You look hot and uncomfortable. Not the best beachwear."

He was looking at her uniform.

"I'm on my lunch break. I don't usually come to the beach dressed like this."

"I like it when you wear a lot less than that."

Kate couldn't help smiling at that, but threw his hand back

143

at him and stood up.

"Some people have to earn money."

He stood up and put his hands up in the air in surrender. "I'm sorry, my parents have money. They don't allow me to gain useful employment."

"I have to get back to work."

"Can I walk with you?"

"No, best not."

"You're ashamed of me!"

"I have to get back!" she said, with feigned impatience.

"Can I at least tell you why I came? Barbecue at ours Wednesday night."

"Wednesday? A work night? Ah…but you wouldn't know about that."

"It's the last week of August. How much more of this weather are we going to have?"

"Good point."

"You'll come?"

Kate nodded and he leaned down and kissed her lips, pausing for just a second, the tip of his tongue touching her teeth. Then he reversed away from her, stepping into the cold frilly waves. He waved and walked off in the direction of the harbour. She watched him go with confused feelings. He was a sweet boy and she liked him a lot. She didn't want to hurt him.

Now wasn't a good time to be starting any kind of relationship

Not when she'd decided to leave Exmouth and go and live in London.

NINETEEN

Exeter was busy. Kate had bought a few things and was feeling tired. She went to a cashpoint and withdrew money. Then she headed for a coffee bar and sat down, placing her bags on the seat opposite. She drank her coffee and stared through the window at people walking by. Her eyes followed a young woman passing, in a hurry, patting at her hair. Kate touched her own hair. For most of the first year of university it had been short and blonde but then she had allowed it to revert to its natural colour and had grown it. It sat on her shoulders and was easy to manage. When she moved to London she would have to have it cut and styled.

There were other things she would need to do. It wasn't just a case of dressing up, having a new wardrobe or different hairstyle. In order to establish a life somewhere else she would need a place to stay. She'd already looked on the web at house shares, focusing on the section where people sublet their rooms for short periods. A couple of places appealed to her. One for two months and one for six weeks. Both of them sounded as though they needed someone urgently; that way there would be less chance for them to investigate references.

In less than a week she would be in a B&B in London going to see the short lets and starting a new life. All she needed was a new identity.

Before getting the bus back to Exmouth, she went into a bookshop to buy an A–Z of London. She walked around the non-fiction section and found a small paperback edition. Holding it in her hand she drifted a little, browsing the displays and the shelves. She found herself drawn towards the cookery section. There were piles of cookery books everywhere, many of them discounted, with photos on the front of chefs who had become celebrities.

Kate had a sudden memory of sitting in a kitchen in Croydon with Rosie, who she had lived with for nearly nine months two years before. Rosie's kitchen had been the hub of her flat. Even though it was tiny everything happened there. There was always some baking going on, the smell of cooking wafting through the rooms. Kate's favourite had been Rosie's biscuits and her fairy cakes which her mother, Kathy, an Irish woman, called *wee buns*. They sat in tiny pleated paper cups, smaller than muffins, only a couple of mouthfuls of warm sponge topped with butter icing. It only took Rosie a moment to throw some eggs, flour and sugar into a bowl and mix it as Kate (Alice, then) separated the pleated paper cases, ready for the mix to be spooned in.

Kate picked up one of the glossy hardback books on the table in front of her. It was heavy, substantial, hundreds of recipes and photographs of dishes. On the cover was an attractive young woman, her hair carelessly pulled up on top in a bun, strands of it escaping and curling round her jaw. *COOKING IN A HURRY!* was the title.

Rosie never hurried when she cooked. Rosie never hurried anything.

Kate felt her throat stiffen. Rosie was in the past. They had been close, but although Rosie had said that she would come and visit Kate at university once she was settled in, she never had. She'd written some letters (*I prefer this to the dreaded emails!*). She'd sent her a birthday card and a poetry book (*My favourite poet when I was a young woman*). She'd explained how busy she'd been and how nervous she was to make any contact in case someone followed her and found out about her new identity (*I'd hate to be the cause of any disruption to your new life*).

Kate had smiled at this. As if someone would *still* be watching Rosie. In the end she'd decided to visit her the previous year, during her first summer break. It was a trip that she'd wished she never taken.

Kate got off the train at Croydon. It was a hot day and she felt overdressed in jeans. She combed her fingers through her hair, feeling the stiffness of the mousse she'd used. It was longer now than when she'd lived with Rosie. She was also wearing her glasses, black frames with no prescription lenses. It had been a disguise that she had liked. Over her shoulder was a bag which held her sleeping things and a change of clothes. She was hoping to stay over at Rosie's. She left the station and walked for a few moments, pausing outside a coffee bar. It was the place where she had worked for some months while living at Rosie's. In a year it had changed completely. It was no longer called The Coffee Pot. It had been taken over by a coffee chain and had tables and chairs out on the pavement. She walked on along the high road. It was Saturday lunchtime and the streets were quite busy. People were no doubt heading for the shopping centre. She kept going until she saw Rosie's street. A feeling of anticipation was building up inside her. She wondered what Rosie would say. *My goodness, Kate, is it really you!* She knew she would hug her because that's what Rosie was like. Right from the first moment they met Rosie gave her a bear hug. *You've lost weight! Aren't you feeding yourself down at university?* she might say. She would bring her up to the flat fussing all the time and pull her into the kitchen and the kettle would come on and the biscuits would come out. *I'm still baking. Really I should be on a diet, Alice. I've put on loads of weight.* She might call her *Alice* by mistake, but that was all right because it would only be the two of them.

Kate had reached the corner of Rosie's street. She walked along it, a spring in her step. A woman came out of a house on the other side. It was someone Rosie had nodded to whenever she saw her and Kate hesitated, knowing that she could be recognised. The woman walked past her though without a glance.

She went on, feeling pleased. At Rosie's door she rang the bell. There was no answer. She rang it again and glanced at the adjacent door, the flat beneath Rosie's. Kate wondered who lived there now.

There was no sound at all from Rosie's flat, no footsteps coming down the stairs. Rosie was out. Kate frowned. She'd not considered that possibility. Why not? It was Saturday, there were any number of places where people went on a Saturday.

But Kate had relied on the fact that Rosie mostly liked to stay in. Her work as a social worker was draining and she had always said that she needed a day to recover. She could usually be found watching the various cookery programmes on a Saturday morning, her feet curled under her on the sofa.

Kate moved away from the door and began to walk back up the street. Just then she saw a familiar figure turn the corner. She smiled, knowing it was Rosie straight away because of the clothes. A long full skirt and a loose blouse over the top. The colours clashed but Kate knew Rosie would not care about that. She took a deep breath and waited, anticipating Rosie's change of expression when she saw her.

But Rosie had stopped and turned around as if someone had called her name. Seconds later she was joined by a teenage girl. Kate was about thirty metres away so she couldn't hear what was being said but she could hear the tone of the conversation. Rosie was making little exclamations, surprised and delighted. The teenager was talking rapidly, holding out bags to show Rosie. They started to walk down the street and Kate saw the teenage girl slip her arm through Rosie's so that the two of them were joined, walking in unison.

Kate felt something dark flutter in her chest.

It was clear in a second. Rosie had another girl living her; a foster placement; a teenage girl who needed a home. *The girls who come to me are either mad, bad or sad*, Rosie had once said, only half as a joke. Kate had been bad; a girl who had killed another child. She had found refuge in Rosie's big skirts. Which was this girl? *Sad*? Abused at home, needing space to finish her studies? Was she *mad*? Anorexic? Depressed? Rosie was an island where such girls could go. There was a van across the road and Kate headed for it. She stood beside it and pretended to be looking at her phone as Rosie and the girl passed on the other side. Rosie didn't look round; she was too absorbed in what the girl was saying. Kate could hear her now.

What time is Kathy coming round? Did you say seven? And then we'll order the takeaway. That way I can show Kathy my new things before we eat. And she's bringing the photos of Majorca. I can't wait to see them but I bet I look a sight with that sunburn! I want to put a couple on Facebook. You should come on Facebook, Rosie. It's where everyone's meeting people now. That way you can get to know new people....

The two of them turned into the path up to Rosie's flat. Kate watched as their backs disappeared through the front door. It closed and she exhaled as if she'd been holding her breath for a long time. Kathy, Rosie's mother, had an apartment in Majorca. She had asked Kate to go too, but she had never had the chance as this girl had.

After a few moments Kate walked back to the station, bought a coffee and got on a train heading out of Croydon.

Now Kate was waiting in a queue to pay for the A–Z. She was feeling tired and looking forward to getting back to the house and having a rest. She got the cash out for the book and as she handed it over she was startled by a small pile of paperbacks on the counter next to the till.

Children Who Kill, by Sara Wright.

She put her hand out and touched the cover. She had this very book at home, buried under some clothes in a drawer.

"Card payment?" the sales assistant said.

"No, cash…"

"That book is half price with any purchase over ten pounds."

The sales assistant smiled apologetically. Her A–Z only cost £7.99.

"That's OK, I didn't want it," Kate said, handing over the money.

"It's actually pretty popular. I guess it's the lurid title. Grabs your attention. Plus we have the writer giving a talk on it tomorrow evening at seven."

Kate frowned. Sara Wright would be here in Exeter?

"Promotional tour. I guess her publishers are keen to sell it."

"Thanks," Kate said.

She took her purchase and walked towards the exit. She thought of the last time she'd seen Sara Wright in Rosie's flat. Then she'd been wearing a suit and looking thin and tall and sharp. Kate had never much liked her. When she found out who she really was she'd felt a mixture of fear and rage towards her. Now, her book was finished and she was edging into Kate's life again.

Maybe Kate should write a review of it. Tell her what *she* thought of the story of Jennifer Jones.

TWENTY

Kate was about to get changed in order to go out. She had half an eye on the television set in her room as she chose something to wear. The local news was on and there was an item about Jodie Mills. She stood very still and watched the presenter say that a local man had been arrested and charged with her murder. The police were not releasing the man's name, the presenter said, but local sources had named him as forty-two-year-old Martin Johnson who worked in one of the caravan parks on Sandy Bay. This information made Kate sit down on the side of her bed, her shoulders tense.

Did it make it any better, knowing who had murdered Jodie Mills? It did for the family, Kate was sure. Maybe it also made the community feel safer knowing that this man had been arrested and charged.

It should have made Kate feel better but it didn't. She should have felt a moment's delight knowing that the police would realise that they had been too hasty, that they had trampled all over her life because of something she had done in the past. There would be no apology, DI Lauren Heart had made that clear. Kate slumped back on the bed. She plucked at the duvet and grabbed at the corners, pulling them round her so that she was covered up. She knew that the police would consider themselves entirely justified. She pictured DC Simon Kelsey, his hair gelled stiff at the front, like wire; his sneering voice in her ear, *You're no stranger to a crime scene.* How would he react to the news? Most likely he would shrug off the memory. What was it to him? Another day's work and in the end they had arrested and charged someone. What would it matter to him that Kate's little world had been shaken?

And yet how could she even think about *her* pain against the murder of a nine-year-old girl? Was this to be her future? Living in the shadow of *two* dead girls? She closed her eyes and turned over, pulling the duvet with her.

The barbecue was well under way when Kate arrived.

"Sorry, I forgot the time," she said, breathless.

"No matter," Jimmy said and pulled her through the house to the back garden.

His housemates and other friends were sitting on a variety of chairs and cushions. Someone had strung fairy lights across the back of the house and there was a home-made barbecue on the patio, bricks stacked in a circle and what looked like the tray from the grill across the top of it. A coffee table was alongside it with paper plates and a kitchen roll for napkins. Jimmy did speedy introductions. The new girl, Karen, was there and she smiled at her. The smell of meat cooking was strong and Kate realised that she was hungry.

"I walked past the tourist information office today. I didn't see you there," Jimmy said.

"I had the afternoon off. I was in Exeter, shopping."

"Is this what you bought?" He looked down at her clothes.

"No! These jeans are old and so is this top!"

"So you dressed up in your oldest clothes to come and see me?"

He was grinning. She tried to straighten the hem of her T-shirt. It was wonky. She should have changed but after the television news she hadn't the heart to do it.

"Still looks good to me."

He reached across and ran his finger down the side seam. It gave her a tingle across her chest. She gulped down some beer.

"I needed a few things. I'm going away for a couple of weeks with some university friends," she said. "Camping in Exmoor."

"Two weeks? You never said," he said.

"It was a last-minute thing."

"But I saw you yesterday. You didn't mention it then."

"I still wasn't sure then."

"Oh, right…"

He seemed put out. Kate knew she had hurt him.

"Someone dropped out," she said, softly. "Everything's paid for so I said *Why not?*"

Jimmy seemed about to say something else but they were joined by a young man with a can of beer at his mouth. He was unsteady. It looked as though he'd been drinking all afternoon.

"What have you heard from young Becky?" he said, ignoring Kate's presence.

"Not much," Jimmy said, looking awkward. "She says it's freezing cold on the island and the wind blows in four directions at once."

154

"That's Scotland for you. When's she coming back?"

"After Christmas."

"You and her? Getting back together?"

"No!"

Jimmy looked at Kate, his hands out in a helpless gesture. "Col," he called, "come and take Rob away from me in case I do him some damage!"

"Point taken. I've opened my mouth in front of this young lady. I've put my foot in it."

Col appeared, looking harassed, a long-handled spatula in his hand.

"Come on, Rob. There's a deckchair over here with your name on it."

"Sorry," Jimmy said.

A couple got up off some cushions that were on the grass. Jimmy took Kate's hand and pulled her over and they sat down. Kate had her back against the garden fence. It felt cooler there, further away from the barbecue. There was food cooking and she wondered whether to get some. She was comfortable though, her hand cupping the cold beer can. The garden seemed darker here, the fairy lights shining brighter. She felt relaxed, comfortable, her earlier thoughts about Jodie Mills receding.

"The holiday was a really good deal," she said, gently.

"It sounds great. And we can meet up when you come back."

"Yeah, sure."

She felt bad. Why was she spinning this story to him? In a couple of weeks he would know it had all been made up. Maybe it would have been kinder to end it with him.

"Sorry about Rob and his big mouth."

"That's all right. You don't have to apologise about him mentioning Becky. I don't mind you talking about your ex-girlfriend."

"OK, I'll talk about her, but you tell me about your first serious boyfriend first."

"Why?"

"It's only fair."

"It's not a game," she said. "We're not teenagers! *You tell me about your first kiss and I'll tell you about mine!*"

She'd used a silly voice. He looked away, sheepish. She'd hurt his feelings.

"Sorry…his name was Frankie. He was in the last year of his degree and I was just about to come here. He was great, in all sorts of ways. He looked after me, sort of, but…"

Jimmy was looking into the darkness but she could tell he was listening.

"He wanted me to do my degree where he was. He wanted me to change my plans and I wanted to come here so it didn't work out."

"How long were you together?"

"About six months."

"But it was serious, though? You and this Frankie?"

"I suppose you could say it was serious."

"You were in love with him?"

"This is the third degree!" Kate said, smiling, trying to lighten the atmosphere.

"Did he give you the pendant?"

Kate remembered the chain and the heart, flat and smooth, the name *Alice* engraved on it, which had broken off her neck and dropped into Jimmy's bed. He took her silence for confirmation that Frankie had given it to her.

"How come it had the name *Alice* on it?"

"My middle name. He liked it. It was a kind of secret between us," she lied. "Now tell me about Becky."

He shook his head. "I'm done talking about Becky. She's out of my life now."

"You tricked me! Can I at least see a photo of her? To see what I'm being compared with?"

She'd already seen a photo of Becky in the passport she had looked at. She was curious to see her away from the stiff pose that was required.

"Later. I've got some in my drawer, in my room."

"What makes you think I'm going into your room later?"

"I wasn't assuming, I mean… I didn't mean *for* anything…"

"It's OK. I was joking. You can show me pictures of your girlfriend later. When I'm in your room."

"Chicken wings!" Col called from the barbecue.

"I'm hungry," she said, "Let's eat."

Much later she was lying on his bed. She still had her jeans and top on although Jimmy had taken his shirt off. She was flat on her back but Jimmy was on his side, his knee across her stomach. The room was dark but they'd left the curtains open and the streetlight was shining in. From outside in the hall she could hear footsteps and hushed voices as the last of Jimmy's friends left the house. It was almost eleven.

"I have to go soon," she said. "I've got work tomorrow."

"I'm sorry we didn't…you know…It was just that I was afraid someone would bang on the door. That's the problem

157

with having a bedroom downstairs."

"I don't only want you for your body," she said.

"That's a relief," he said, "because now I've got to go and clear up. That was the deal. Col did the barbecue. I clear it all up."

She sat up. "What about the photo of Becky you were going to show me?"

"Oh yeah."

He swung his feet off the bed and opened the drawer. Kate noted that the photo was nearby, handy to get out, to look at. She wondered if he was over this girl at all.

"Here."

He switched on the bedside light. Kate looked at it. She smiled immediately.

"She looks like me," she said. "Is that why I attracted you? Because we look similar?"

Jimmy went to answer but then stopped himself.

"I was going to say no," he said, after a moment. "But maybe, in a way, that's right. It's not so much that you're her double, but you are of a type."

"This is getting worse!" she said, almost laughing.

"No, what I mean is I was attracted to her maybe for the same reasons I'm attracted to you. She was quite forthright and knew her own mind. She was outgoing. She had darkish hair and was pretty. She was bright. I guess I saw a lot of those things in you."

"All this at first glance?"

"No, at first glance I saw the hair and the face and, yes, maybe you did remind me of her. But I liked the rest as well."

"And this girl broke your heart?"

158

"I never said that."

"True though."

"I'm over it. Look, are you going to keep me talking all night? I've got to walk you home and then start clearing up the stuff from the barbecue."

"You don't need to walk me home."

"I do. Let me go and check that there aren't any plates or glasses outside. Then I'll lock up and walk you back. It doesn't matter how late I go to bed. I don't have to get up for work, remember?"

She watched as he pulled on a shirt and went out of the room. She heard him mumbling in the hallway, talking quietly to someone. She took another look at the photo on his bedside table. There was no doubt that he still had feelings for this Becky. It made her feel less bad about leaving him. She opened his top drawer and replaced the picture. Then she stood up and listened carefully in case he was coming back. There was no sound though so she guessed he was out in the garden.

She stepped across to the plastic boxes of Becky's stuff that were stacked in the alcove. She lifted the lid of the top one and pulled out the file that said *Rebecca Andrews Papers*. She opened it and slipped out the passport. Then she flicked through the rest of the things in the folder and found a photocopy of a job application. It was dated a couple of years before but there, on the top right-hand corner, was a national insurance number. She looked round for a paper and a pen but couldn't see any near at hand so she took out the photocopy, folded it up and slid it into the passport and put both of them into her bag.

She replaced the folder in the plastic box.

She was putting her shoes on when Jimmy came back in.

"Ready to go?" he said.

"Sure."

He kissed her on the mouth and she wondered, fleetingly, if he was thinking of Becky when he did it. A tiny part of her hoped he wasn't.

TWENTY-ONE

Kate got to the bookshop in Exeter a little late for Sara Wright's talk and then made a decision not to go in at all. Across the road was a branch of HMV and she headed for it. She spent some time in the DVD section, looking at the rows of films and box sets. She selected a film called *The Big Sleep*. She'd heard of the novel that it came from and knew that it was a crime classic. Would Jimmy already have it? She doubted it. He mostly had box sets and recent movies. This was made in 1946 which made it virtually an antique.

After she paid for it she walked to a cashpoint and withdrew some money. Then she headed back towards the bookshop.

When she got to the place where Sara Wright was just finishing her talk she was pleased to see that there wasn't a large audience. She counted about twenty people sitting on chairs. This calmed her, making her think that *Jennifer Jones* wasn't headline news any more.

Sara was sitting at a table. She hadn't changed in the two years since Kate had seen her. Her hair was still short and she was wearing a smart jacket and trousers even though it was a warm night. She had coloured bangles on; Kate could see them shifting about as she moved her hand up and down.

There was a queue of people holding their books. Sara smiled up at each of them and opened each book so that she could sign it. A couple got into conversation with her and she talked to them, gesticulating with her hands, one of them holding a pen ready to sign. Kate wasn't really sure why she'd come. Curiosity perhaps. Anger maybe. The journalist had been the reason why the life she had had with Rosie had come to an abrupt halt. Studying for her degree at Sussex and having Frankie as her boyfriend had all been snatched away from her because of this woman's desire to write about her in the newspaper she was working for. That day, at work, Kate had become quite puffed up about this; now though she felt oddly flat. If it hadn't been her maybe it would have been someone else. Maybe it was always going to be only a matter of time before she was exposed.

Her current situation was just as precarious. Only her probation team were supposed to know her true identity but now there was DI Lauren Heart, DC Simon Kelsey and DC Pat Knight. Would they keep quiet about her? Would they really not go home to their husbands, wives, or partners and say *Guess who I met today?*

Kate decided to join the end of the queue. In her bag she had her copy of *Children Who Kill*. As she waited, Sara Wright chatted to the person a few people in front of her. Her voice had a sweetness to it, as if in total contrast to the dark content of the book she'd written. Kate had no intention of reading the book. Would Sara recognise her? Two years before she had had short cropped hair. She had worn no make-up, dressed plainly. She'd wanted to fit in, to be part of the crowd, not to stand out in any way. And now? Wasn't she just the same? Her hair was longer but she wore the clothes of a student. She looked like hundreds of other young people milling around Exeter. The only time she looked a bit different was when she was wearing her uniform for the tourist information office. Her polyester blouse and skirt and her badge that said *Kate*.

Then she was behind the person who was speaking to Sara.

Anxiety gripped her. Was this the right thing to do? She had no time to think about it because the person in front got her book signed and walked off without a word of conversation and she was faced with Sara Wright. The journalist beamed a smile up at her and she handed her book over.

"Who shall I sign this for?" she said, looking down at the book.

There had been no recognition. No moment of surprise. Kate felt a sense of disappointment. Was it because she looked so different or was it because Sara Wright simply thought her another book buyer and hadn't even bothered to look at her face?

When Kate didn't answer she looked up again.

"Shall I just sign it *Best Wishes*?" she said.

"You could put *Alice*," Kate said.

"Right…" Sara's eyes stayed on Kate's face for a few seconds. Then she looked down at the book.

"If it's not too much trouble you could put my second name as well. Alice *Tully*."

Sara stopped writing and looked up at her. She sat back in the chair, her shoulders dropping.

"Alice," she said, softly. "Surely the last person in the world I expected to see."

***

They went to the coffee bar that was in the bookshop. Sara bought the drinks and sat opposite her. Kate stared around the café. There were people there who had been in the talk. They were giving little smiles in Sara's direction. Sara followed Kate's eyes. They didn't speak for a few moments. It was as if they were sizing each other up.

"I've had some surprises in my life but this beats them all," Sara said. "What's your name now?"

"Kate Rickman. I live along the coast from here. My university is here. I go back for my final year in September."

Sara nodded, blowing on her coffee. She looked like she was considering her reply and Kate realised what she'd said: *I go back for my final year in September.* It was as if she really meant to do it, as if she hadn't made plans to run away.

"Is it OK if I call you Kate?"

"Sure."

"Have you read the book?"

Kate shook her head.

"I hope my being here hasn't upset you too much."

"No."

"I did extensive research for the book, Kate. I have shown it to people who work in the field of law and they say it's a good addition to understanding why crimes like this happen."

"Who did you show it to?"

"A couple of barrister friends of mine, a professor of criminology who I correspond with, a couple of probation officers who sometimes write articles on prison reform matters."

"The police?"

She shook her head. "The police don't see this kind of study as helpful to their role. They catch criminals. They're not interested in *why* they did something. That's for other people to sort out."

"So the book, for you, wasn't just about making money, making a name for yourself?"

"This book hasn't made me much money. Nor will it. I did it because I was gripped by the case. I wanted to understand."

"And write about it in your newspaper."

"It's how I used to make my living. It was my job."

"You don't do it any more?"

"I work for television news now."

"Television? A promotion? You got a promotion after ruining my life?"

"No, I won't accept that. I wanted to write a serious piece about you which did not reveal your identity. Someone in my office saw a way to make a few quid and they released the information to the tabloids. I am very sorry for what happened, but I won't take the blame."

Kate exhaled and rolled her eyes. Sara looked uncomfortable. She seemed to be on the brink of responding but chewed at her lip instead.

"I did my best to protect you…"

"If you'd never come in the first place –"

"Then I would never have written this book, and I happen to believe that this book will lend some understanding to what happened at Berwick Waters."

"I know what happened there."

165

"It's not all about you, Kate."

"Course not. Michelle and her family…"

Whatever righteousness Kate managed to summon up it was always deflated by the mention of the Livingstones. Michelle's death hovered over her, an albatross, ready to pluck, to scratch.

"I wasn't just referring to the Livingstone family. This crime had wider reverberations. If you read my book you would see. It affected the lives of many people. The children at the school you went to needed bereavement counselling; the head teacher was admonished for not forwarding records to social services and had to retire early. Your social worker was suspended for not making contact after you moved to Berwick. The local police were ticked off for ignoring reports from neighbours that your mother was working as a prostitute and using her house to entertain men."

Kate flinched at the word. "My mother was not a prostitute. She was a model."

Sara went on as if Kate hadn't spoken. "Lucy Bussell's family were hit badly. Her brothers had the worst of it. Even though they were not at Berwick Waters and the incident had nothing to do with them it was their possessions that were found at the lake; the *weapon* belonged to them. Their survival games, their activities, were viewed as strange aberrant behaviour. The press acted as though *they* should take some blame. The brothers foolishly spoke to journalists and showed them their belongings, the military stuff. They boasted a little and were treated like minor celebrities but really they were just being judged, tried and convicted of being oddballs."

Kate frowned. She had never liked the Bussell brothers.

"And if they'd not had their things up at the lake…" Sara said.

"There would have been no weapon."

Sara shrugged. Kate tried hard to remember. If there had been no baseball bat might she have picked up something else?

"Lucy Bussell went into foster care and so did her brother Joe. Separately. The older brother, Stevie, was unemployed and lived in a hostel. When Mrs Bussell was well enough she and Lucy and Joe lived together as a family. Stevie joined them. They lived like that for a few years. Joe left college and got some apprenticeship work but then, months later, inexplicably, he committed suicide."

Kate sat forward, alarmed. "Because of what happened at the lake?"

"I don't think so. I spoke to Mrs Bussell when I was researching the book. This took place two years ago. A long time after the business at the lake. Mrs Bussell said he was depressed."

"I didn't know."

"No reason why you should."

Kate pictured Joe as she remembered him in Berwick. He'd been fourteen or so then, big for his age, always wearing army combats. His brother Stevie was much older but smaller and leaner. They were a nasty pair, she remembered. Now she might view them as idiots but as a ten-year-old girl there had been something *dangerous* about them. She wanted to ask how Joe had committed suicide but it seemed prurient.

"So, you see, the book is about the wider effects of the crime."

Kate frowned. "Are you saying that these things happened because of me?"

"No. Cause and effect are never easy to pin down. The

whole thing didn't start with Michelle's death. Maybe it started much earlier. Maybe Michelle's death was as much a result of other things as was that of Joe Bussell. That's the kind of stuff I've written in the book, Kate. Why not read it? Before you judge me."

Sara's phone beeped. She looked at it. Then she pulled her bag off the floor and dropped it in.

"The Livingstones moved to Scotland. They live just outside Edinburgh. They had another child, I believe, a boy," Sara said even though Kate hadn't asked. "I have to go now, but here's my card... You can call me whenever or email me. Best to use your new name. If I can ever be of any help to you, Kate, I will."

She placed a card on the table. It was dark pink and had the words *Sara Wright, Journalist* in bold italics. Kate picked it up. Underneath was her address, *1, North Street, Angel, Islington.* The word *Angel* made her think of churches and graveyards.

"Goodbye, Kate."

She watched Sara walk away. She put the card in her bag and then continued to drink her lukewarm coffee. She thought about Joe Bussell who hadn't been in her mind for eight years. Had she ever, once, thought about him? She doubted it. Now he was dead. And Lucy, in her letter, hadn't mentioned a word about it.

TWENTY-TWO

When the tourist information office closed on Saturday afternoon Kate flopped down in a chair exhausted. Grace, who still seemed to have lots of energy, was tidying up the leaflet displays. Moments later Aimee emerged from the staff area holding a tray on which there were three elaborate cupcakes. Kate couldn't help but smile when she saw them. They were small works of art. Swirls of icing topped with what looked like mini marshmallows and silver balls. Grace clapped excitedly.

"This is to say goodbye, Kate," Aimee said. "You've been really hard-working and we've loved having you here, isn't that right, Grace?"

"It certainly is. We'll miss you!"

"And here's a small gift from Grace and me!"

Aimee held a package out in her hands. Kate took it, feeling embarrassed.

"Open it!" Aimee said, picking up her cupcake and taking a bite.

It was a mug. It felt like porcelain and had a curved side like a tulip. It was a dusky pink colour. Kate threaded her fingers through the handle.

"It's great," she said.

"And when you're back from camping, come in and have a cup of tea with us. We won't be so busy then and you can tell us all about it."

"I will," she said, looking away, feeling emotional all of a sudden.

"When are you off to Exmoor?" Aimee said, pulling at the paper encasing her cupcake.

"Tomorrow morning. I'm meeting my friends at Taunton. One of them has a car."

"Two weeks in a tent!"

"Yeah, I'm looking forward to it."

"Rather you than me. I like a nice hotel. En-suite facilities. If I had the money I'd go to Spain tomorrow!"

Aimee's eyes had a faraway look as though she was imagining herself on a plane. Then she seemed to collect herself. She pointed to the plate.

"Eat your cake," she said. "It cost a small fortune!"

On her way home Kate stopped at a cash machine. The sun was shining but there was a chill breeze coming off the sea. She queued behind a group of teenage boys in patterned shorts and flip flops. They were talking about the evening ahead, the bands who were playing at the harbour as part of the bank holiday weekend festivities. One of the boys was swigging from a bottle of beer. Another was staring at the screen of his mobile phone, complaining *Every five minutes my mum texts me! It's driving me nuts!* She watched them walk off, one pushing the other so that he had to step off the pavement onto the road.

Some teenage girls across the way squealed and shouted to them and then continued to do so across the slow-moving cars.

Kate withdrew cash and pushed it into her back pocket. As she walked up the incline towards her road the noise of the town grew quieter. Now that she was away from the seafront she felt warm. Gulls were squawking, swooping from roof to roof, a couple on the ground tearing at a bag that they'd plucked from a rubbish bin. Turning back she looked at the sea and could see the ferry making its way out of the harbour. The water glistened in the late afternoon sun.

She felt an aching sense of loss. She had lived here for six months and in Exeter for eighteen months. She loved being near the sea. In the winter it was quiet, the beach looking vast and empty; the people walking their dogs seeming tiny and lost in the landscape. Sometimes the sea looked solid and hard, as if you could walk on it. Then there were days when it appeared to roll from side to side and other times when it broke apart with creamy cracks. In the summer it always seemed tame, dotted with boats and jet skis, speedboats, wind surfers and swimmers.

She would miss seeing it every day.

She liked the house she lived in with Sally and Ruth and even Robbie who never seemed to go home and was always frying an egg or making toast when she wanted to do something in the kitchen.

She had a boyfriend, no matter that he carried a torch for someone else. He felt something for her she could tell. And she felt easy being with him.

Now she was going to leave it all behind.

Back at home she moved around her room, wearily checking that she'd packed the right things. She pushed the cash she'd withdrawn into the front zip compartment of her rucksack where the rest of her money was. Then she slipped her box of antidepressants alongside it. On the floor was her holdall in which she'd packed her laptop and papers and the books she wanted to take with her. The rest of her belongings would stay here until Sally and Ruth decided what to do with them. Maybe Julia Masters would arrange to have them boxed up.

She felt weak all of a sudden, her legs rubbery. She wanted to lie down but there was a knock on the door.

"Hi!" Sally poked her head in. "Can I come in?"

"Sure."

Sally sat on the corner of Kate's bed. She looked at the packed bags.

"All done?"

"Mostly."

"You sure you don't want to come to this party tonight? It was an open invitation and all you'd need is a bottle of wine. Lots of interesting people there."

"I'm going down to the beach with Jimmy and his housemates."

"It'll be cold!"

"I'll dress up warm, Mum."

"Oh, don't. Why am I always trying to *mother* people. Sorry."

"I don't mind."

"How was the last day at work?"

"It was good, but I'm glad it's all over."

"Not long till college starts again. Almost as soon as you're back from camping."

172

"I know," Kate said, fiddling with her rucksack.

Sally's eye settled on her holdall that was on the floor.

"You're taking a lot of stuff with you!"

"Just warm stuff. It's cold on the moor. That's what my friends say."

"Fancy spending two weeks out in the elements. How will you manage all this? Do you want me to come to the station with you in the morning?"

"No, thanks – I'll be all right!"

"OK, OK, I'm leaving before I tell you to brush your teeth before you go to bed. Come in and say goodbye to me in the morning. Doesn't matter how early."

The door closed behind her.

One day, in a couple of weeks, Sally would walk into her room concerned because she hadn't come back from her camping holiday. She'd look among her things and wonder what had happened to her. She would most definitely go to the police and inform them about a missing person. Then they would discover that there had been no camping trip.

Sally would feel cheated, lied to.

And how long would it take for this information to filter through to other people? To Julia Masters? Jill Newton? Rosie? She pictured them all, one by one, stopping what they were doing as news reached them, whether by phone or email. Jennifer Jones had disappeared. And the police detective, Lauren Heart, perhaps she would nod and say, *I thought she might do something like this.*

But Kate wouldn't be there to hear any of it. She would be living in London and her name would be *Rebecca Andrews*.

She'd dressed warmly, wearing jeans and a hooded top. She knew the beach often got chilly quickly on summer nights. Jimmy was wearing a short-sleeved T-shirt and was shivering. He kept saying he wasn't cold but Kate didn't believe it. His housemates were a few metres away talking to a group of girls who had just arrived and were carrying cans of beer.

It was past ten o'clock and they were sitting on a couple of towels, their backs against the sea wall. They were among thirty or so other young people all packed on the small area of the beach that was closest to the harbour. The lights along the front lit up the black sky with a haze of colours and the sound of music from the band on the harbour gave the place a party atmosphere.

Kate and Jimmy were drinking the last of a bottle of wine. Jimmy had gulped his down but Kate was sipping hers, her eyes staring into the darkness of the sea. The tide was coming in, the water lapping closer, the sound of the surf only just apparent during gaps in the music. Jimmy was rubbing her arm and she felt momentarily happy.

"Have I already said thanksh for the movie?"

"You have, several times."

"Course I've seen *The Big Shleep* on television years ago. It's a total classic."

"I know. That's why I bought it."

"It was really influ…influ…"

Jimmy had been drinking for a long time. When she'd got to his house that evening he already looked a bit unsteady on his feet. He'd been ridiculously pleased with her gift and had wanted to watch it there and then. She'd been keen to go on the beach though, to feel the fresh evening air.

"You mean it was really *influential*."

He nodded. Kate finished her drink. She was feeling content. There was a kind of warmth inside her. Jimmy's head was on her shoulder and it felt nice to be there. She nudged him.

"Why don't we go up onto the harbour and get some chips. It'll be warmer up there."

"Great idea," he slurred.

"Maybe we can get you a cup of coffee, to wake you up."

"Even better idea. We could go back to ours and watch the movie."

"Maybe," she said, rolling up the towels, sticking them into her bag.

As they walked up the steps of the beach she thought of something.

Why not stay? Why leave Exmouth at all?

The idea made her feel heady. There was a sensation of lightness in her chest. The business with the little girl, Jodie Mills, was over. She would probably never see those police officers again. Why go when she didn't really need to?

They walked along the esplanade towards the docks. The music was louder, the lights brighter. People were walking aimlessly, some holding hands, others deep in conversation. They passed a line of girls singing. It contrasted with the beat of the rock band on the harbour but she hung onto the sound, sweet and harmonious. She began to sing herself, under her breath, a feeling of well-being pulsing through her. This was her place now. Kate Rickman, third-year undergraduate; home town, Exmouth.

They came up to a coffee shop and Kate steered Jimmy towards it.

"I'll have a coffee, too," she said.

He went inside and she walked away back towards the sea wall and leaned against it. She'd done nothing so far that she couldn't undo. The money she'd taken from the bank could be re-deposited. She could return Rebecca Andrews' papers without Jimmy ever knowing that they'd been taken in the first place. She could wake up tomorrow morning unwell, say she was going to go camping later in the week. Then she could make excuses, cry off the whole holiday saying that she'd got cold feet. Sally and Ruth might laugh at her but that didn't matter. Sally, in her motherly way, would be secretly pleased that she wasn't going out and sleeping in the *elements*. Jimmy would be happy. Maybe he would even think that it was a sign of Kate's feelings for him that she couldn't bear to go away on holiday without him.

She could stay in Exmouth. Why not?

She realised that the band had stopped playing and she could hear bits of conversations from nearby and the sound of other music coming from one of the nearby restaurants. Jimmy was in the queue inside the coffee shop. He was leaning precariously to one side. She wondered if she should go in and make sure he was all right. Exactly how much had he had to drink?

"Hello!"

She felt a tap on her shoulder. She turned round and saw a familiar face. It was DC Simon Kelsey. Her mood darkened and she took a step back away from him. She frowned at him, puzzled as to why he was there. He looked different to when she'd seen him before. Then he'd been in a suit, shirt and tie. Now he was wearing jeans and a sweatshirt. His hair was still gelled through, little arrows poking up from his forehead. He came towards her.

"Fancy seeing you, Kate. Or is it Jennifer? Which would you prefer me to use?"

"Why are you here?"

"Came for one of the bands. I know the drummer. Had no idea I'd run into you, Jennifer. But then you do live here, don't you?"

"Leave me alone."

She turned away from him, staring rigidly into the coffee shop. At the edge of her vision she thought she could see some other young men looking across at them, pointing, saying things. One of them was laughing.

"Jennifer, you shouldn't be off with me. You've nothing to fear from me now. Not now that we've charged the gardener."

The word *gardener* threw her. She was confused.

"What?"

"Martin Johnson, gardener. Worked along the coast at the caravan parks and other attractions. He probably made friends with the little girl during the week so that when he saw her down on the beach on the Friday night it was too good a chance for him to pass up."

Kate didn't answer. She took a couple of steps away as the music started up again, loud and raucous. Simon Kelsey followed her though and then leaned closer to her, his mouth near to her ear, his hand resting lightly on her waist.

"Still, it gave me a chance to get to know you, Jennifer.

Maybe we could spend time together. I've always wondered what it would be like to kiss a girl who's killed someone…"

She pushed him away.

"Coffee," a voice came from behind her.

Jimmy was standing with two cardboard cups looking a little fresher than he had ten minutes before.

"Bye, Jennifer," Simon Kelsey said. "Be seeing you around!"

He walked off back to his friends. A couple of them patted him on the shoulder and looked back towards Kate.

"Who was that?" Jimmy said.

"Don't know." Kate whispered the words.

"Why'd he call you Jennifer?"

"Just some out-of-control drunk," she said.

"Shall we get some chips?" Jimmy said, handing her one of the cups.

When she got home it was past midnight. She was sober and her face was cold. She sat on the bed and looked at her packed bags. She thought she might cry; she'd felt on the brink of tears for the last couple of hours.

Instead she got undressed and got under the duvet and set the alarm on her phone. She had a train to catch and she didn't want to miss it.

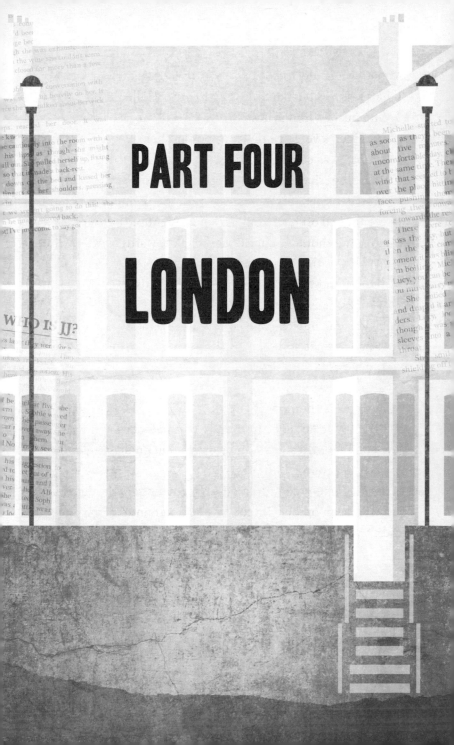

PART FOUR

LONDON

TWENTY-THREE

The bed and breakfast was in Finsbury Park, north London.

When Kate walked into the room she felt immediately hemmed in. There was a single bed and a chest of drawers with a small television on top of it. The en-suite was tiny, a shower and a toilet sandwiched in together. The woman who had showed her there was already on her way back downstairs.

She'd spent time in small rooms like this before.

She put her bags down on the bed and sat down. She picked up the remote and clicked the television on. It was seven o'clock in the evening. Her train had broken down and it had taken her most of the day to get there. The long, slow journey had felt as though she was in a kind of no man's land. Once in north London she could start to sort herself out.

She made herself get up and unpack. She only planned to stay there for a few days. She had arrangements to make and the most pressing one was to get a sublet, even if only for a few weeks so that she could have an address and get a bank account. She unzipped her rucksack and took out the wad of money that was there. She'd taken some out of her bank account each day for the last couple of weeks and now it had to pay her way until she got a job. There was more than fifteen hundred pounds on the bed. This was money that she'd saved since coming to Exeter.

Twice, in the past, she'd started her life again with a new identity. Both times the arrangements had been made by other people. She'd never had a passport because she wasn't allowed to leave the country, but she'd had everything else; bank account, NHS card, national insurance number, details of schools she'd attended, examination certificates. Anything she'd needed had been provided. But it all came at a cost and she didn't want that any more.

Now she had to find these things for herself.

She had Rebecca Andrews' passport and this would be the key to getting other things. She had to brush aside the feelings of guilt she had about taking it from Jimmy's room. She had to set up a Hotmail account in Rebecca Andrews' name and contact some of the sublets advertised on the web. And she needed to eat. Possibly she would get some replies by tomorrow morning and arrange visits.

Her mobile phone lay on the bed where it had slid out of her rucksack. She knew she couldn't turn it on because that might lead to her being traced. Even though no one was looking for her she didn't want to leave an electronic trail of any sort. She should get rid of it and buy a pay-as-you-go phone. She couldn't quite bring herself to let it go yet though, so she pushed it down into her bag and packed other things on top of it.

She'd bought a money belt and she put it on under her T-shirt with the money inside. Then she went out of the B&B and walked around, familiarising herself with the area. It was on a busy road and there was a bus stop nearby. She glanced down the information panel and saw that there was a bus that went directly to Wood Green. Further up, towards the tube station, she found an internet café. It took her a while but she set up a Hotmail account as Becky90. She bought a slice of pizza and ate it while she went onto a couple of the sublet sites she had found. She found the adverts she had seen the previous week and contacted both of them, saying she urgently needed a short-term let.

The next morning, when she returned to the café, there was a reply from one of the sublets.

Hi Becky. I'm going away on Saturday for six weeks and would LOVE to let my room. Come and see it Monday evening at seven.

There was an address underneath, in Archway, north London. She looked it up in her A–Z. It was a little further out than she'd wanted but it would be only be for six weeks and so she'd have time to look for somewhere else.

She replied, *See you at seven tonight!* Then she typed *Becky*.

In her holdall she had a couple of references she had forged from addresses of student houses she'd known around Exeter. She hoped these would be sufficient.

She had enough money to get her through the first weeks in London but she urgently needed to get a job. Rebecca Andrews' national insurance number would help with that. Once she was in a more long-term let she would have until January before Rebecca Andrews returned from her Scottish island dig and perhaps needed to replace her missing papers. Then she could slip abroad; lose herself in Spain, work in the bars and restaurants for the summer.

Then she would be by the sea again. After that? She didn't know.

She logged on to an employment agency's website. There were forms to fill in. She ticked the boxes and gave what information she could. At the bottom there was a space to write a kind of statement. She filled it in briefly but clearly.

> *Rebecca Andrews*
> *Nineteen years old*
> *British citizen*
> *Dropped out of my university degree course for financial reasons*
> *I've never had a job so have no references*
> *I'll do anything; office, shop, restaurant, bar work*
> *Yes, I'll do cleaning jobs*
> *I don't mind antisocial hours*
> *I don't have a mobile at the moment but am getting one and will let you have the number*

After she'd logged off she bought a roll and some fruit. She took it into Finsbury Park and sat on a bench to eat it. The sun was out and it was warm and the park had a parched look. There were criss-crossing grey tarmac paths that matched the greyness of the buildings outside. Everyone seemed to have more clothes on than she was used to. In the summer, at the seaside, people tended to shed their clothes even if often it wasn't really warm enough. Here, even though it was warm, there were cardigans and jackets and long trousers and skirts.

She wondered where people went when they wanted to swim.

She finished her drink and went back out onto the streets. She paused by the bus stop just as one was approaching and saw that it stopped at Wood Green underground station. On an impulse she jumped on it. She sat up the back as the bus made its way through heavy traffic.

She took her A–Z out of her bag. She'd marked the page where Lucy Bussell's home was in Wood Green. The tube station was very close, a short walk; Lucy had said that in her letter. Kate saw from the map that Wood Green station was coming up soon. She hopped off at the stop and looked across at the station and tried to pinpoint exactly where she was on the map.

It only took five or so minutes to find Lucy's street. She went along it until she came to the right number.

She walked up the path to the porch. There were three bells. One of them said *Alexander*, the name Lucy had signed her letter with. She hesitated, wondering whether to ring it or not.

"Can I help you?" a voice came from behind.

She turned and saw Stevie Bussell standing at the end of the path with a woman who had her arm through his. She would have recognised him anywhere. He hadn't changed at all. He was shorter than the woman but his chest was broad. He was wearing a short-sleeved T-shirt over jeans and the muscles at the top of his arms stood out. The army clothes had gone. The woman was carrying some shopping bags and was all smiles. They both had dark glasses on even though it was a little overcast.

"I was just looking for Lucy," Kate said. "I said I'd call round."

Stevie took his sunglasses off as if to see her better. He looked at her curiously.

"We just saw her in the high street," the woman said. "She was going to McDonald's. Didn't she say that, luv?"

Stevie nodded.

"I'll catch her there," Kate said.

She walked past them without another look. She carried on along the street, a feeling of unease settling on her. She had a sense that Stevie was watching her walk away. She couldn't help but turn her head to see. There was no one there though. They'd both gone inside the house.

She carried on, her feet slowing down. She was at a loss as to what to do. She'd not had a very firm plan in coming and had drifted towards Lucy's house. She decided to find somewhere to buy a pay-as-you-go phone. Then she could ring Lucy and make an arrangement to meet her somewhere. Hadn't she said, in her letter, *If you're ever in London call by and see me.*

She walked across the high street and headed along the shopping area. It didn't take her long to find a phone store and buy the phone. She went back to the bus stop and stood in the shelter, staring at the passing traffic. It was just after four. She had the rest of the day to get through. Time, in London, seemed to move slowly.

A familiar face crossed the road towards her. It took her a few moments to realise that it was Lucy Bussell. She was *sure* it was. She recognised her from the tiny photo she had sent. She was on her own and cutting in between cars that were queuing at the lights. She had skinny jeans on and an oversized top. She looked very thin, her cheekbones standing out. She seemed to be heading straight for her and Kate had a bizarre thought. Was she coming to see her? But no, how could she? Lucy had no idea that she was coming or what she looked like.

Lucy swept past the bus stop though and let out a shriek at a boy who was standing along the pavement. There was some rapid talking but Kate couldn't catch what was being said. The boy was tall and skinny and had a very tight leather jacket on. He looked as if he was too warm but the leather jacket was stylish. Then they both turned and walked past the bus stop in the direction of Lucy's street.

She watched them go, the boy's arm around Lucy's shoulder, Lucy's hand hooked over the belt of his jeans.

Lucy Bussell, it seemed, had come a long way from the eight-year-old girl that she'd known in Berwick.

TWENTY-FOUR

Kate took her new phone back to the B&B and put it on charge. Then she had a shower. The water was lukewarm and came in spurts but it felt good to wash her hair. The towel was small and thin and barely dried her. She got dressed again, keeping the towel wrapped around her hair so that it would dry quickly.

She thought about Stevie Bussell. He and his brother Joe had always been together. Then, when she lived in Berwick, Stevie was eighteen and seemed to have no other friends than his younger brother, Joe, who was fourteen. Joe should have gone to a special needs school and Stevie should have been at work but the two of them seemed to hang around the village all day pretending to be soldiers. In contrast to his brother and his sister, Lucy, Joe had been big, hefty, like a grown man. Stevie always looked weedy beside him. Today he hadn't looked weedy. He'd clearly done some fitness training. Kate wondered what he did now. Today, Monday, mid-afternoon, he was out shopping with his girlfriend, whose name, Kate remembered, was Terri.

She hadn't liked the way he'd taken his sunglasses off and looked at her but then Stevie had always made her feel uncomfortable. When she was ten and walking along the lane outside their houses he would put his hands up to his eyes in the shape of binoculars as if she was some kind of prey and he was hunting her.

Then there was the way he spoke about her mother.

How's your mum?

The three words were innocuous enough – a polite enquiry coming from anyone else – but Stevie always meant something quite different. Even as a young girl she had known that. She remembered him from years before, lounging back on the grass, maybe in the local park or at Berwick Waters. He'd been wearing his camouflage combats, ugly green clothes that were slightly too big for him. When he opened his mouth she heard the words *How's your mum?* In her mind she saw him lick his lips and place his hand over his crotch as he said it.

Kate cringed with shame.

She would not think about it. She pulled the towel off her head and began to comb through her wet hair, slowly, carefully, in case there were any knots. She looked in the tiny mirror that was on the wall. After she'd combed and combed it she sat very still, her shoulders rigid, her hair still wet, unable to block out entirely her memories.

Carol Jones, her mother, the model. Sometimes Kate (Jennifer, then) lived with her, sometimes she was placed with other people; her gran, various childminders and sometimes foster placements. When she did live with her mother she had to be grateful for whatever time her mother allotted to her. There was always something more important for Carol Jones to do and it usually involved a camera. All she ever wanted was to appear in glossy magazines but in reality she lived from week to week doing low-paid jobs or collecting benefits. Just about every concrete memory Kate had of her mother centred on a photograph of some sort. She lay back on the bed, her wet hair on the pillow, and thought back to when she lived in the cottage on Water Lane.

It was the Easter holidays and Jennifer was watching her mother getting ready to go out. Her mother had just got out of the shower and was wearing her dressing gown. She took it off and stood naked in front of the mirror. She seemed to stare at herself for what seemed like a long time. Jennifer looked over at her mother's thin body, her small breasts and flat stomach. Her mother caught her eye and smiled.

"Not bad for a woman who's had a baby!" she said, laying her hands flat on her abdomen.

Her mother was humming a tune, flicking through her clothes as she decided what to wear. Jennifer was thinking of other things. She was wondering what she and Michelle would do today. They might take a walk through the town and look at some of the DVDs in the Co-op. Jennifer had money so they could buy some sweets and drinks and spend some time in the park. Some of the other kids from their class might turn up.

"Which one, Jen?" Her mum's voice interrupted her thoughts.

Her mother was standing holding a flimsy white blouse up in front of her. In the other hand she had a red jumper with a deep V-neck. Jennifer pointed to the red jumper. The colour suited her. It contrasted with her hair.

"Did I tell you about this photographer, Jen? His name's Mr

Cottis. He's freelance and he said he might be able to act as an agent for me. That's been my trouble all down the line. I never had an agent. I never had anyone to fight for jobs for me. If Mr Cottis likes my work enough, then who knows what'll turn up."

Jennifer smiled at her mother. She wondered whether to ring Michelle to see what time they were going out. The fact that she lived next door made this seem like an odd idea but at least she would know when to be ready.

"He's sending a cab for me. For ten. God, it's twenty to, I need to get a move on. You'll be all right by yourself, won't you, Jen?"

Jennifer nodded. She wouldn't be by herself. She'd be with Michelle. Maybe Michelle's mum would let them do some baking. Jennifer liked making cakes, even if Michelle was a bit grumpy about it.

When her mum had finished dressing Jennifer went downstairs and into the living room. She looked out the window and waited for the cab to come. She could hear her mum moving around upstairs. She was still singing which was a good sign. She could hear the spraying of the lacquer can and the tapping of her mother's heels on the ceiling above. Then she heard a door shutting and her mother coming down the stairs. It had just gone ten o'clock.

"Any sign of the cab, Jen?"

"No."

There was a strong smell of perfume as her mother came into the living room. She stretched across Jennifer and pulled the curtain back. Then she sat down on the armchair, her legs crossed, her ankles tucked neatly together.

"How do I look?" she said.

"Really nice," Jennifer said.

They waited. At ten fifteen her mum got up and went out to the front door. Jennifer heard it opening and saw her go along the path and look up and down the lane. She came back in making tsking sounds. Jennifer heard her pick up the telephone and make a call. After a terse conversation she put her head into the living room.

"Obviously been some mix-up with the arrangements," she said.

She went upstairs again, her footsteps heavier than when she came down. Jennifer sat in the living room for a while. After half past ten she followed her up. She stood on the landing and listened to the sound of crying, of nose blowing.

"Are you all right, Mum?" she called.

"Go away, Jen."

There was a knock on the front door. She went down and opened it to find Michelle standing there. Her hair had been done differently; bits at the front had been plaited and pulled back with pretty slides.

"Are you coming out?" she said.

Michelle looked past her as she almost always did when calling for her. After seeing her mother's portfolio Michelle viewed Carol Jones as almost famous and loved to catch a glimpse of her.

"I'm not sure. Mum's…"

The sound of her mother's voice came down the stairs. "Is that the cab, Jen?"

"No," she called up.

Her mum's bedroom door slammed and Jennifer smiled at Michelle.

"I'll call you later. Mum needs me right now."

Michelle's face dropped. "I could come in. We could dress up in some of your mum's clothes."

"Not today."

Michelle exhaled a long noisy sigh. Then she turned and walked off without a word. Jennifer closed the door and stood against it. She looked up the stairwell, dark and empty. Maybe her mum's new agent would send a cab for her later.

Mr Cottis took a lot of photographs of her mother. Somehow they got into the hands of the Bussell brothers. Kate remembered the day of Lucy Bussell's birthday party when they had all gone up to Berwick Waters. Stevie's comments had enraged her then. Now when she thought back she wondered if her mother had done more than have her photographs taken. Stevie Bussell had said that she was a *prozzie*. He'd said that she had *blokes visiting her every day*.

Kate felt her throat constrict. Her hair, wet and clammy, stuck to her face as she blinked out tears. She wiped them away with the heel of her hand. She sat up and sorted out her clothes. Her mother was not a prostitute. She would not sell herself for money. She was a model. Wasn't she?

She got up and washed her face and got dressed. She had to keep busy. She put the money belt on under a shirt. The mobile phone was still charging. Maybe, when she got back from Archway, the phone would be ready to use and she could send a text to Lucy Bussell.

TWENTY-FIVE

Kate got to Archway quicker than she'd thought and so she went into a café by the tube exit and ordered a toasted sandwich and a drink. The doors of the café were wedged open and outside the traffic edged past, a number of cyclists weaving in and out between lorries and cars. It was still warm and the atmosphere was smoky, the tang of petrol fumes thickening the air.

She wondered what the weather was like in Exmouth. She pictured the esplanade, the curve of the bay and the palm trees that fringed the beach. There was traffic there, lots of it, but it was always dwarfed by the vastness of the sky and the sea. She thought about the tourist information office. Aimee had told her that the numbers of visitors dropped dramatically after the bank holiday. Visiting families no longer came because of the end of the school holidays, so much of the trade was older couples or surfers or walkers passing through. She imagined Aimee leaning on the counter staring out of the windows at the streets, tapping her fingers. Perhaps she would be moaning to Grace about her ex-husband and his cavalier way of looking after their daughter, Louise.

She thought of the Mills family; they had come to Sandy Bay for a holiday and would go back home without their daughter, Jodie. Even though it had nothing whatsoever to do with her it gave her an uneasy feeling; as if giving the badge to the toddler had somehow brought bad luck on the family.

She pictured the girl, Jodie Mills, when she was in the shop. She had been messing around with their leaflets then singing a pop song over and over. She had drawn attention to herself and then snatched the badge off the toddler, as if she wanted everyone to see what she had done. Her mother and father looked harassed. Her brother stood outside the door as if to distance himself from the lot of them.

Families were a mystery to Kate.

Michelle Livingstone's mother and father came into her head.

Sara Wright had said they had moved to Scotland and they had had another child, a boy. She began to form pictures of them. Mrs Livingstone, her hair red and curly like Michelle's. She worked as the school secretary and was always in the corridors of the school carrying files and papers with her. Mr Livingstone (*call me Frank*) was cheerful whenever she came into contact with him, always making little jokes. Kate felt sore at the memory of them. She crossed her arms and stared through the window as the traffic stopped and started, stopped and started. The long days in the courtroom came into her head. The big room had bright lights that made her squint a little. It was packed with people and every day she had to look around for a long time before she picked Michelle's parents out. They didn't always sit in the same place and sometimes it was a while before she could find them. In all the days that she sat in the court they never looked her way, not once. It was as if she wasn't there; as if she didn't exist.

She felt herself shrink down in the chair. The air in the cafe was heavy; the pungency of the traffic had forced its way in. Her head seem to loll on her neck as if she had no control over it. She put her palm up to her forehead to hold it firm. Thinking about those days was always dangerous. She *had* to live in the present. She *was* Becky Andrews.

She paid her bill and walked away from Archway station. Using her A–Z she looked at the street names and found the one she wanted. It was almost seven. She was still feeling a little shaken when she rang the bell at the house. The front door opened instantly.

"Hi, you Becky?" a girl said.

Kate nodded.

"Come in. I'm Petra. I've just this minute got in from work. Come through to the kitchen. I'll get you a drink. Tea? Coffee? Cold drink?"

"Some water would be nice," Kate said, stepping past two bikes that were lined up in the hall.

Petra was wearing shorts and ankle-length canvas boots. Over the top she had a silky jacket that looked way too big for her. Her hair was cropped and she had a number of hoop earrings in one ear.

Kate sat at a table in the kitchen. At first glance the place made her heart sink. It was messy. The table had small piles of papers and magazines and some stacked dishes that were clean but hadn't been put away. The work surfaces had foodstuffs sitting out, cereal packets and jars of jam and peanut butter.

There was a pile of unwashed breakfast plates waiting by the side of the sink. Kate felt her stomach turn slightly at the sight of it. Petra got a glass from a cupboard and reached across the mess to fill it with water.

"It's not that tidy a house," she said as if reading Kate's mind. "But everyone's really friendly."

She put the glass on the table. "I'll show you my room in a minute. Thing about this house is that it's big. Seven bedrooms, a kitchen, living room, two bathrooms and an extra toilet out in the garden, would you believe! It's owned by Greg, this ex-student who's fiftyish and has been working on this PhD on Samuel Beckett for about twenty years. This is how he supports himself. There are actually nine people who live here because two of the rooms are rented by couples. So it's a big place and some of us come and go. We stay here for a while and then go off travelling and if there's a free room when we come back we return. Like, last year? I was in California for six months. When I came back one of the lads was leaving to go to Australia for a year so I took his room."

Kate nodded, her eyes wandering round the room and taking in the mess that was everywhere. Petra watched her as she did.

"Kind of explains why things are a bit chaotic down here. But it suits the people who live here. We can pay our rent weekly if we like and Greg is pretty understanding about money. If you're looking for a home from home this probably *isn't* the best place to come and stay. If you're looking for a short stay and you don't mind a bit of mess this is OK. There's always the chance that when I come back someone else will be travelling off somewhere and you might have their room. That's if the place hasn't driven you mad by then. The other really good thing about it is that it's cheap. In relation to London prices, that is."

Kate started to relax. She was beginning to realise that this would be a perfect place for her. People coming and going. No time for anyone to start asking her any questions.

"What's your story, Becky? Why are you looking for a short let?"

"I've just deferred my university course for a year. I was in a relationship but that ended and I wanted a break from the guy. I thought I'd spend a bit of time in London. See if I like it."

"That's funny. I had a boyfriend like that. I left him in Hoddeston. Where you from originally?"

"Norwich."

"I thought there was a bit of an accent there. Where were you at university?"

"Exeter."

Kate was brief and to the point. She didn't elaborate in case it sounded as though she was trying to persuade someone of the truth of her story.

"Come up to my room. I'm on the top floor."

She followed Petra up the winding stairs. There were boxes on each landing with names scrawled on them in felt tip. Some of the doors of the rooms were open and she could hear music or voices coming out. At one door Petra stopped and banged on it.

"Brian, washing up. It's your turn."

A mumbled voice came back and they headed up the stairs to the top floor.

198

Petra took a Chubb key from her pocket and opened her room door.

"I like my room locked."

It was a contrast to what she'd seen downstairs. It was spacious and had a bay window. There was a double bed and a huge wardrobe and chest of drawers.

"That wardrobe and chest of drawers will be full of my stuff; clothes, books, bedding, general belongings. So your stuff will have go somewhere else. My advice is to buy a rail and some storage boxes. There's room enough for them. What do you think?"

"It's OK. It's good."

"Look, it won't kill me if I don't sublet it, but if I do it gives me a bit of extra cash."

"I want it," Kate said. "Great! You said you had references?"

"Sure."

Kate got her references out of her bag and handed them to Petra. "They're photocopies."

"That's all right. I can keep these? Show them to Greg?"

"Of course."

"OK. I'll ring you when I've spoken to him. Then I need a deposit. A couple of hundred quid and say two weeks' rent in advance. How's that?"

"That's fine."

"OK, I'll be in touch."

"As soon as you can? I'd be grateful. Otherwise I need to go see some other places."

"I'll let you know tomorrow. I'll email."

Kate walked away from the house feeling positive. This could work. She could use Petra's room and maybe, when Petra came back, she might be able to get another. She got on the tube, thinking about the practicalities. It would take a chunk out of her money but first thing the next day she would go back to the job agency and give them her new phone number. If Petra said she could have the room she could easily get a rail and some boxes. She had very little luggage so wouldn't need a lot.

It was short term. It would give her a place to breathe.

All she had to do was wait and see what answer Petra gave her.

She got back to Finsbury Park. She bought some fruit juice and bananas and headed back to the B&B. When she got in she could see that the mobile phone had charged. She found Lucy Bussell's letter and keyed her number into the phone. She sent a message.

I'm in London and you said in your letter to come and see you. Could we meet? I'm staying in a B&B at Finsbury Park. We could maybe have a pizza or something? Are you busy tomorrow lunchtime? Kate

She pressed the *send* button.

Then she locked her room door and got undressed. She put the television on and flicked around the channels. A few moments later she heard a beep. She looked the screen.

Hi Kate! What a surprise! I have some stuff to do tomorrow but could meet you about three? How about the café in Finsbury Park. Lucy

She replied agreeing and saying that she was looking forward to it. As soon as she put the phone down on the bed she felt apprehensive. To meet Lucy again after all this time seemed a *mad* thing to do.

Not more mad than running away and making a new life for herself though.

The next morning Kate visited the employment agency that she'd registered with. She was offered the chance of a job straight away.

"Telephone sales," the man in the agency said. "I sent them your forms and they're very interested. Minimum wage, six-hour shifts. Some in the evenings. They give you one hour's training and start asap?"

"I'll take it," she said. "What do I have to do? Go for an interview?"

"Telephone interview. Sit over at that desk and I'll get them to ring you shortly. You might be able to start tomorrow."

Kate sat for a few minutes and when the phone rang she snatched up the receiver.

"Rebecca Andrews?" a voice said.

She answered with a cringe of guilt. She was pretending to be Jimmy's old girlfriend. What would he think if he ever found out? The interview took no more than ten minutes but it went well. She replaced the telephone and spoke to the man at the desk.

"I start tomorrow at ten."

"Well done."

His words were half-hearted as if he didn't care one way

or another. He took a drink from a Dr Who mug and turned back to his computer. She noticed, at the corner of the desk, a Dalek pen holder.

She headed for the internet café. She bought a coffee and waited a few minutes for a free computer. She went on the news website for Exmouth and double clicked on the site with some apprehension. She half expected to see herself as headline news: Convicted Child Killer Goes Missing. It was a ridiculous expectation because everyone she knew thought she was on a two-week holiday to Exmoor. It would be another ten days or so before anyone realised that she was actually gone. Her eyes scanned the page anyway. There was an item about the Jodie Mills murder.

Caravan Park Recruits Extra Security Staff
In an effort to allay the fears of families extra security personnel have been taken on at Sandy Bay for the remaining days of the high season. A spokesman said, "While we recognise that visitor numbers will be dropping with the end of holiday season we still feel it's important to increase levels of security in the bay and surrounding area. All efforts will be made to make holidaymakers feel safe."

There was also an item about the bank holiday weekend.

Sunshine Brings Visitors to Exmouth
Visitor Numbers Break New Records: Exmouth saw visitors streaming into the town at the weekend enjoying the

festivities and soaking up the fine weather. Town Councillor Mark Williams said, "We are particularly pleased with the innovative use of the docks as a music venue. It attracted younger holidaymakers. It's important that Exmouth caters for all ages." The councillor added, "We are of course mindful of the recent tragedy at Sandy Bay."

Kate sat back. She missed being at Exmouth. She'd only been gone a couple of days but it was the knowledge she was never going back that was hitting her. In just under two weeks' time it would become official. Kate Rickman, aka Jennifer Jones, had left for good. She wondered whether it would make the press. Every other thing that had happened to her had found its way into a newspaper. There was no reason why this would be any different. She closed the Exmouth website and then accessed her emails and found one from Petra.

Becky, you can have the room. Bring the deposit and rent around on Thursday night. You can move in on Saturday. Petra

She sat back and smiled. She had a job and a room.

And this afternoon she was going to see Lucy Bussell.

Things were looking up.

TWENTY-SIX

Kate was late getting to the café at Finsbury Park. She'd been trying on clothes to see what looked best. She didn't have many things with her but she was unsure what to wear. She wanted to appear relaxed and natural and yet she was feeling neither of these things. Lucy Bussell was a sixteen-year-old girl who'd just finished her GCSEs. Kate wasn't much older but she felt as if she belonged to a different generation.

She decided on some skinny jeans and a loose top. She looked at herself critically in the mirror. At some point, when it came to using the passport to get a bank account, she would have to cut her hair, just so that she looked more like the photo of Rebecca Andrews. But for now it was still long and straggly. She gathered it together at the back of her neck and pinned it up. She put some lipstick on. Then moments later, after frowning at herself, she got a tissue and wiped it off.

She was being ridiculous. It was a meeting with a girl she hadn't seen for a long time. It wasn't a *date*. She delved into her rucksack and pulled out the book by Sara Wright she'd brought from Exmouth, put it into her bag and left.

Lucy Bussell was already there when she arrived. Kate saw her straight away, sitting on her own at a table by the window. The only other people in the cafe were a couple of mums and toddlers. Lucy was staring at her phone and was deep in thought. It gave Kate a chance to look her over. She was slight but her hair was big, probably moussed so that it was full on top. She was wearing deep red lipstick which made her skin look pale, almost white. She had on a denim jacket over a short skirt. She suddenly looked up as if she knew someone was scrutinising her. She frowned a little uncertainly. Kate smiled and walked towards her.

"Lucy," she said. "Sorry I'm a bit late."

"No, I'm early. Stevie dropped me off on his way to work."

Kate took the chair opposite. Lucy sat up straight and looked a little shy. With her fingers she pulled at strands of her hair at the front. There were two cans of Coke on the table and unused glasses.

"I got you a drink," she said.

"Thanks, that's nice of you."

"I hope you like Coke?"

"I do. Thank you."

Kate picked a can up and pulled the metal ring back. She poured it slowly, tilting the glass to the side. Then she took a mouthful. Lucy hadn't touched hers yet. She looked sheepishly at Kate. There was an awkward silence and eventually Lucy picked up her Coke and edged the ring pull back and sipped straight from the can.

"They're bad for you, really. Sugary drinks…" Lucy said, between sips.

"Are you sure you didn't mind me sending you that letter?" Kate said, more abruptly than she meant to.

"No, course not…"

"I was worried that it might have upset you."

'No. I was *surprised*. I mean, I haven't thought about all that stuff for a long time. I told you that in my letter and then to hear from you out of the blue…"

"I accidentally discovered your address – it's a long story – but once I'd got it and had the opportunity to make contact it seemed the right thing to do. It seemed to be something I *had* to do."

"And now you've come to see me!"

"Yes, and I want to say face to face that it was a terrible day at the lake and I am so sorry…"

"There's no need. You said that in the letter."

"I know but…"

"It was a long time ago. We were just children."

"Yes, we were."

Little Lucy Bussell was trying to put her at her ease; it made her feel emotional. She hadn't always been kind to Lucy when they were *just children*.

"After it all happened you went into foster care," Kate said after a moment.

"For a while. My mum was ill. Then when she was better I lived with her again. We changed our name. Because of the publicity."

"And Joe went into foster care?"

"He did. Then we all lived together again. Stevie came now and then."

There was music playing in the cafe, Kate realised. It was orchestral, some tune that she'd heard before, but it was so low she could hardly make it out. One of the mothers was reading a story to her toddler. The child was making excited noises and trying to turn the page before the mother had finished reading it. Kate looked back to Lucy. She was fiddling with a bracelet. She looked underweight, as though it was only her clothes that were giving her shape.

"Lucy, I only recently heard about your brother Joe and what happened to him. I'm so sorry."

Lucy pulled at the front of her hair. She pushed the can of Coke away to the furthest edge of the table. It looked like it might topple off.

"Did you read it in the newspapers?" she said, a hint of anger in her voice. "They used a terrible headline. YOUNG MAN FOUND HANGING IN RAILWAY SIDINGS. And then just a couple of sentences. Really brief. It should have had more."

Her eyes glistened. Kate was dismayed. She put her hand out and covered Lucy's. It felt small and fragile. She thought of what Sara Wright had said about the press hounding the Bussell brothers after Berwick Waters, portraying them as oddballs. Then they had been happy to print lots of stuff about them. She wondered if Lucy had seen any of that. She doubted it. She had only been eight, living with foster carers; they wouldn't have let her see the newspapers.

"I'm so sorry for you and your mum and your brother."

Lucy took her hand away and pulled a wad of tissues from the pocket of her denim jacket.

Kate had never known Joe, always seen him as weird. Was his suicide just a random thing or did it have roots in the things that happened at Berwick? This thought had weighed on her since she had spoken to Sara Wright. Could it be that she, in some way, was responsible for *that* as well? Joe had gone to college though and after that had got an apprenticeship. Had he changed from that strange boy in combats? Had he become a regular guy? And if so, why had he taken his own life? These were things Kate wanted to ask Lucy but didn't feel she could.

"Did you get your GCSE results?" she said, changing the subject.

"One A, two Bs and five Cs," Lucy said, blowing her nose.

"That's really good. What was the A?"

"Art. The results mean I can do A levels and maybe go to university. I mean, I'm not sure if I *want* to go to university, but at least I've got the choice now. Stevie says it's a waste but I don't listen to him. My boyfriend, Donny – I think I mentioned him in the letter I sent – he says you absolutely have to go to university. Especially for art."

"I thought you'd broken up with Donny?"

"That was all a misunderstanding. There was a girl at school who just spread gossip and it wasn't true but I believed it like an absolute idiot!"

"Well, that's good!"

"You got a boyfriend?"

"Sort of. In Exmouth."

Kate had her mouth open as if she might say more, explain about moving to London, but she made a quick decision to keep that information to herself. Lucy knew she lived in Exmouth and knew her name was Kate. It didn't hurt to talk about her Exmouth life.

"What's his name? How long have you been seeing him?"

"Jimmy, his name's Jimmy. I've not been seeing him long but he's a nice guy. He's big into crime films and box sets..."

Kate faltered on those words, sensing an irony she hadn't picked up on before. Jimmy loved his crime. What would he say if he knew who he'd been spending time with? But then crime series and movies were not real life, nothing like it.

"Do you think it might be serious?"

"I don't know. I do like him... What about you and Donny?"

"Oh, definitely. He's the one. I've liked him for years and years. Even when he used to go out with a girl called Jude. She was in my class and it seemed like they were never apart. But then he split up with her and now it's me and him. Stevie doesn't like him much, but it's not his choice, is it?"

"No. It's your choice."

The door opened then and two women came in, one fanning herself with a magazine, the other getting her purse out and heading for the counter. Kate noticed some nice-looking cakes and pastries on the counter.

"Would you like a slice of cake?" she asked.

Lucy shook her head. "Thing is, since Joe's death, Stevie looks out for me. I think, maybe, he feels that he should have been around more for Joe? So now he's always asking me what I'm doing, where I'm going, who I'm seeing...."

"You didn't tell him you were seeing me?" Kate said, alarmed.

"Oh no, he just thinks I'm meeting a friend from school. But that's the problem. He feels he has to know everything about my life. Donny says I should tell him to mind his own business but…you know…he's my brother."

"Where does he work?"

"He's a security guard. In a shopping centre."

Kate pictured Stevie immediately. In a uniform. His muscular arms covered up, a peaked cap on his head. Not a soldier but someone who sensed a bit of status, if only guarding clothes shops and restaurants.

"Oh, one other thing," Kate said, reaching into her bag. "This was sent to me a few weeks ago by a journalist. I think she may have spoken to your mother a while ago? Well, the book's out now…"

"I've seen it. She sent a copy to my mum."

"Have you read it?"

Lucy shook her head. "Have you?"

"No. The journalist said it was a serious piece of work but the title…"

The book lay on the table. *CHILDREN WHO KILL*.

"It's like that headline about my brother," Lucy said, after a moment. "It's what sells papers and books."

"I know."

Lucy frowned, her face clouding over. Kate waited, sure she had something she wanted to say. She'd pulled Sara Wright's book towards her and was staring at the cover.

"Joe was making a go of things. He'd done all right in college and the apprenticeship was going well. That's what my mum said. He used to work lots of overtime, said he really wanted to learn the job, be successful. Then he came home from work one Friday and seemed a bit fed up. He said he was going out for a

210

drink with his mates and we never saw him again. They found him a couple of days later hanging behind Kings Cross station. The policeman said he probably did it like that because he didn't want someone in his family to find him. He was thinking of us…"

"Oh, Lucy…"

"Donny says that that maybe Joe was depressed, like, you know, the illness. *Depression*. And none of us knew. Donny has a friend whose sister tried to kill herself and then they gave her these tablets."

"Antidepressants," Kate said, thinking of the slim packet she had in her rucksack, the tablet she took every day, the way it had cleared some of the fog out of her life.

"Yeah, but no one knew. He just kept it all inside."

Kate didn't know what to say. Lucy finished her Coke.

"Anyway, I should go," she said. "I said I'd meet Donny at Wood Green. He's got this summer job in Argos."

They both stood up. Kate, who was small anyway, looked down on Lucy.

"I'll walk you to the bus stop," she said, "It's close to my B&B."

They left the café and walked through Finsbury Park. There were groups of people sitting and lying on the grass and a dog scampering round trying to get hold of a frisbee that was skittering along in the breeze. Out of the park the traffic reared up in front of them. They crossed the road and headed for the bus stop. Kate could see a bus further up in the stationary traffic. It was the one that stopped at Wood Green. It would take a few moments for it to edge towards them.

"We should stay in touch, Kate. You could write me another letter and I'll reply. I've never had letters from anyone! You've

211

got my address."

"Sure I will. And I'm sorry I upset you by talking about Joe."

"I *like* talking about Joe. No one else does. Mum never mentions him, neither does Stevie. If he hadn't died he might be working for himself now, in a proper job."

"What was his apprenticeship?"

"Photography. He was working for my uncle? Kenny Cottis. You knew him, didn't you? I think your mum did some work for him. Oh, I remember now, he took those photographs of your mum and you got really upset."

"Mr Cottis?" Kate said, taken aback.

"I shouldn't have mentioned it. He's not really my uncle though, he's my mum's friend, but he's always been there to help out and when Joe wanted to do photography he'd said he'd teach him the job. He lives near us. Alexandra Palace. Well, it's not *that* near, but it's close enough."

The bus was coming closer but Kate was suddenly back at Berwick Waters, eight years before. Little Lucy Bussell was standing by the side of the lake holding a photograph of her mother, Carol Jones, fashion model, naked. It had been amid the Bussell brothers' belongings, the stuff that they'd buried in a box and kept up at the reservoir so that they could carry out night-time hunting games. The photograph had disgusted her; had sent her into an ugly rage.

"I'm sorry, I've upset you now!" Lucy said, her face screwed up.

But Kate wasn't thinking about her mother now. "Your brother worked for *Mr Cottis*? Learning to take photographs?"

"Yes. Kenny was his boss and tried to help him but… But I don't think he does any of that glamour stuff any more."

212

The bus arrived.

"Have I upset you?" Lucy said, looking concerned.

"No, you get your bus," Kate said with a weak smile.

"You'll write to me again? And I'll reply."

"I will. And remember no one has to know about me seeing you."

"I know."

Lucy got on the bus. It shunted out again into the traffic.

Mr Cottis had given up taking glamour photographs. What about the other types of photographs he liked to take? Those of a young girl dressed up in a school uniform. Had he given up taking those as well?

TWENTY-SEVEN

After Lucy's bus disappeared Kate walked around in an aimless way. A while later she found herself on the parade of shops by the underground station. She saw the internet café she'd used before and stopped abruptly so that a woman behind her bumped into her saying *Sorry, sorry!* She went in and bought a coffee and saw that one of the computers by the window was free. She sat down and felt the heat from the sun. It was like a greenhouse but she paid for an hour anyway and went onto her Hotmail page. Outside, on the street, people walked past the café but she hardly noticed them as she focused on the screen. There was a message from Petra.

> *Hi, Becky! Greg says why don't you come and meet people tomorrow night. He's cooking. We eat at seven. You could bring the deposit then to save you coming on Thursday but it's up to you. Petra xx*

She read it over a couple of times and felt the tension ease.

She would go over there the next evening, meet the people from the house. Maybe she would begin to feel that she really was *Becky Andrews* and that her life was now in Archway, north London.

She wrote an answer and then sat for a moment gazing at the street outside. There were numbers of people passing, probably heading, she thought, for the underground station. Some girls were walking more slowly linking arms, causing annoyance to people in a rush. They seemed deep in conversation and hardly noticed. Behind them, walking with his head down, was a young man wearing shorts but with heavy Dr Marten boots. He headed for a bus stop some metres along. On his back was a rucksack and when he stopped he took it off in a lumbering way, moving his shoulders as if they ached. His gait was slumped and he had a frown on his face as if he was puzzling something out. He looked unhappy.

She pulled the keyboard towards her and typed the words YOUNG MAN FOUND HANGING IN RAILWAY SIDING into the search engine. She saw it immediately. Underneath were a few sentences.

The body of a young man was found yesterday by staff at Kings Cross Station in central London. It was discovered in a largely unused area and had possibly been there for a number of days. A Network Rail spokesman said that the area had recently been fenced off but access had been gained with wire cutters. The spokesman said that it was a tragedy for the young man and his family.

There were a couple of other mentions of what had happened but none of them gave any more details. Kate wondered why the press hadn't picked the story up more widely. According to Sara Wright they had written enough about the Bussells after Berwick Waters. Maybe the name change had hidden the link or maybe Joe Bussell's suicide was not quite such a sensational scoop for them. The article that was there was brief and could easily have been missed. Lucy was right to say that it deserved more than that. She typed in *Joe Alexander*. Several things came up: a member of a boy band, a scientist, a journalist. Then she saw a small local paper article from just eighteen months before.

INQUEST VERDICT OF SUICIDE FOR YOUNG PHOTOGRAPHER

A coroner determined that the death of twenty-year-old Joe Alexander was that of suicide, even though there was no note. His family said that although he was depressed they cannot understand why he took his own life. The coroner felt that the chosen means of death, by hanging, in a particularly inaccessible place, showed a decisive intent on the part of the young man. "This was no spur-of-the moment decision," the coroner said.

Kate sat back, frowning. Joe Bussell made a decision to take his own life. He'd found a place behind a railway station where he could do it. He'd bought wire cutters and gone there to die on his own, knowing that his own family wouldn't be the ones to find him. She remembered him as such an odd boy although she had never once thought about him without his brother at his side. In her mind the two were inextricably joined and loathsome for it. But after what happened at Berwick he had gone into foster care alone and then gone back to live with his mother and sister and Stevie joined them *now and then*. Then he'd gone to college. This all seemed like an improvement.

And yet something made him end his life.

Outside, in the street, the traffic was moving smoothly for once. A woman with a pushchair was pausing by the café window, leaning down to speak her baby.

She thought of Mr Cottis. He was always standing straight and stiff, as though his body couldn't bend if he wanted it to. She typed his name into the computer and afterwards the words *photographer* and *Alexandra Palace*. A listings website came up and halfway down the page was the name *Kenneth Cottis, Portraits and Weddings: Station Road, Alexandra Palace*. There was no website for her to click on, just an address and phone number.

Eight years before, when he visited her mother, he had no office. He had a case full of photographs and equipment that he brought to the house. He came with props and clothes for ten-year old Jennifer to wear. They had sat in a bag in the corner of her room and she'd looked anxiously at them for hours.

There was a squirming feeling in her stomach and she logged off from the computer and sat motionless, staring out of the window, her face rigid and her thoughts heavy. Hadn't she wanted to get away from all this? Hadn't the plan been to see Lucy and say sorry face to face and sympathise with her about the loss of her brother, then move on? A proper new start with no probation officer looking over her shoulder, no local police notified about her presence, no one who knew anything about her. She'd felt the ties that those people had on her, holding her in one place, keeping her on the straight and narrow. *Don't drink too much, Kate. Don't let your grades go down. Make sure you take your antidepressants. Don't think that you deserve any special treatment by the police. Be grateful for the help you've been given. You're luckier than you know.* Kate had wanted to break out of all of these.

But she couldn't be free of the *memories*. She felt them all the time, a thin web that had spun and spun around her. Sometimes they tightened, chafing and squeezing the breath out of her.

She closed her eyes; she *had* to put this stuff behind her.

When she opened them again she focused on the café window and saw a face there. She squinted into the sun and made out a man flat up against the glass looking into the café, his hands cupping the sides of his eyes. A young man who looked familiar. He grinned.

It was Stevie Bussell.

She sat very still, not making any acknowledgement of him. After a few moments he turned his back on her and stood against the glass as though he was waiting for something. She glanced along the street at the bus stop. Could it be a bus? Had he happened to notice the girl who had come calling for his sister the day before? Or could he be just acting stupidly, making faces at people in the café while he was hanging round killing time until his bus came? He had been unpleasant and – yes – he had been stupid when she'd known him before.

She tried to ignore his presence.

She sat for a while glancing at the screen, moving the mouse, clicking on websites. All the time she kept looking up at the window and seeing Stevie Bussell's back solidly between her and the street. Buses came and went and still he stood there. He never looked round once. Was she being oversensitive? He was there for some reason, but not necessarily her. His shoulders moved and she saw that he had taken out his mobile phone and was looking down at it. She relaxed a little. He was making a call. Maybe he was waiting for someone and they hadn't turned up; his girlfriend, Terri, perhaps. The fact that she was in the café and he had seen her there, smiled at her, was nothing more than playfulness with someone he thought he knew.

She was being ridiculous.

A beep sounded. It came from her pocket. She pulled out her mobile phone and looked at the screen. She had a message from an unknown number.

Jennifer, I'm waiting outside to talk to you. You know who I am. Don't make me hang around here too long. Stevie.

Her heart seemed to shrivel. She deleted the message swiftly, as if in doing so she was shoving him away from the café, out of her sight. She stared at the computer screen. She typed a new website into Google, her fingers moving like lead pistons. She read the words on the home page, her mind racing. *Jennifer.* He knew who she was. Had he recognised her yesterday when

219

she was outside his house? Had he known her the moment he set eyes on her?

She slumped back. Her hands were trembling. His back was still squarely against the glass. He wasn't moving. He was waiting for her.

Had Lucy told him?

She got up and pushed the keyboard away. There were people hanging round the counter waiting for space on the computer and she saw one of them move in her direction and pass her. She went out of the door of the café and walked with a straight back, her eyes looking into the distance, ignoring the things and people nearby. She felt him move along with her.

"Jennifer, slow up! You're walking too fast."

She ignored him and quickened her step. She darted out into the traffic and crossed the road between slow-moving cars. He followed her. She felt his hand on her arm and she shook it off. She speeded up but he was still there. When she reached the corner of Finsbury Park she stopped. She did not want him to see her go into the B&B.

"Jennifer, I only want to talk to you!"

"What?" she said.

"Why did you meet with my sister today?"

"I wanted to see her…To…I had things to say to her."

"About what?"

"None of your business!"

She'd raised her voice and some passers-by looked round.

"Calm down. I'm just curious."

"Did Lucy tell you I was here?" she demanded.

He shook his head and got something out of his back

pocket. He handed it to her. She saw an envelope with her handwriting on the front, the name *Lucy Alexander* and her address. She pulled out the page inside it even though she knew what it was. She looked at her own words, written some weeks before.

Dear Lucy,
You will be surprised to receive a letter from me. You may even be alarmed. Please don't be…

"I found this in Lucy's room. I was having a nose around. I worry about my sister, especially as she's hooked up with some no-good guy. I read it and I wondered if you'd come to see her. I waited and yesterday there you were outside my door."

Kate didn't speak. He snatched the letter back from her.

"How did you know I was meeting her? Did she tell you?"

"You sent her a message on her phone. Easy for me to find it."

Kate felt instantly ashamed. She thought that Lucy had told her brother about her. But Lucy had been true to her word. She was decent and nice and yet Kate had immediately suspected her.

"I recognised you as soon as I saw you," Stevie said. "Little Jennifer. You have changed. You look so much like your mum now."

She glared at him. The comment was laced with something. She remembered him from years ago licking his lips.

"What do you want?"

"I just wanted to say hello. What's wrong with that? It's not like we don't have a shared history. You, me and the stuff that

221

happened up at the lake."

"I've got nothing to say to you…" she said and then faltered. "Except, of course, that I'm sorry for your loss… Your brother…"

His face dropped. The swagger was gone. He looked uncomfortable.

"Look after yourself, Miss Jennifer Jones. Or whatever your name is now."

He turned and walked away and she stared after him until he went across the road and towards the tube station. She watched as he disappeared among the crowds. She didn't move, waiting to see if he came back out. After a few minutes, when he didn't reappear, she walked on, past the entrance of the park and towards the B&B. She felt dazed by the encounter. It was too much, too many ghosts from the past crowding around her. It wouldn't surprise her to see the skeletal Mrs Livingstone turn the corner and walk towards her, her piercing eyes seeking her out, pinning her to the spot, looking for atonement.

"Sorry!"

She'd bumped into someone. A man wearing a suit had dropped some files and papers on the ground.

"I'm sorry," she said, bending down to pick them up.

"I should have a briefcase for these," he apologised. "In any case, I think it was me who bumped into you!"

"No problem," she said, walking away, taking one last glance over at the tube station.

When she saw that there was no sign of Stevie Bussell she headed for the B&B and went inside. She went upstairs and when she got into her room she locked the door tightly and stood against it.

TWENTY-EIGHT

Kate got to the house at Archway just after seven. She was carrying three large plastic boxes that she'd bought in a shop near to the tube station. They were different colours, red, white and yellow. It was a special offer; three for the price of two. She was hoping Petra wouldn't mind her storing them in her room. She had enough stuff to carry with her on Saturday.

She was feeling better. She'd had a day answering telephones and while it wasn't the most interesting work she'd ever done, she'd been left on her own to do it and no one had bothered her. She'd got through her calls, one after the other, in a mindless way. Her desk was like a carrel and she was facing a screen on which a script came up every time a phone call was answered. She didn't have to talk to anyone else and say who she was or make any polite conversation. She left her desk to go to the toilet a few times and to have lunch. At five she left.

After the events of the day before she needed the monotony. She needed normal, boring things to happen. She was desperate for time to pass until she could move into the house in Archway. She pressed the doorbell and waited. A window on the first floor was wide open and a head popped out. A young man looked down at her.

"Coming!" a voice shouted from inside the house.

The front door opened and an older man stood there. He was large, chunky and was wearing an Arsenal T-shirt. He pointed a finger at her.

"You must be Becky," he said.

She nodded.

"People usually bring wine to a meal, not packing boxes!" He laughed at his own joke.

"I'm Greg," he said, holding the front door open.

She walked in, a feeling of embarrassment flooding through her. There was the noise of footsteps coming down the stairs and she saw Petra skip along the hallway.

"You've met Greg, then?"

Greg had walked off into the kitchen, still chuckling to himself.

"I wondered if I could leave these boxes here, as long as you don't mind. I've got quite a lot to carry on Saturday."

"Sure. Come upstairs."

"I've also brought the deposit."

"Great."

"Should I have brought wine?"

"No, take no notice of Greg. He's a comedian."

She placed the plastic boxes in the corner of Petra's room. The window was open and a light breeze was coming in. In the bay, on the floor, was a suitcase which was half packed, and a rucksack beside it.

"What time are you going?"

"Got the early flight on Saturday morning. Can't wait."

"Oh, here's the deposit."

"Thanks."

Kate gave her an envelope. "It's cash. That's all right, is it?"

"That's brilliant. Now, why don't we go and eat. Greg can only cook two things. Thai green curry or risotto, but they're both pretty good."

Kate looked back at the plastic boxes before she left the room. The sight of them made her feel good, as if a part of her was already there. Plus she had paid the deposit so things were definitely settled. All she had to do was get through Thursday and Friday in the B&B.

"I love green curry," Kate said, when Greg ladled out a spoonful.

There were five other people at the table. Greg, Petra and three young men, two of whom had headphones on. Peter, the third, was quietly talking to Greg about football. *The Emirates Stadium was the worst decision they ever made!* Greg talked over him, *No, no no! It'll rejuvenate the club.*

The conversation went on and Petra rolled her eyes.

"It is a bit mad here," she said. "But you get used to it."

"Does everyone cook?" Kate said, feeling a moment's sadness, remembering the meals she cooked for Sally and Ruth.

"No. Greg cooks every Wednesday and there's an open invite for anyone who wants to come. The rest of the week we get our own meals. More people usually come but the couple in the back bedroom are on holiday and Suzie, the girl in the next room to me, is going to a work hen party so she couldn't be here."

Kate ate the food. She was hungry.

"So, Kate, what do you do?" Greg said.

The three young men looked up at her, a couple of them frowning as if they hadn't registered her presence.

"I've got a job in telephone sales. It's just temporary."

"So, what do you want to do? With your life, I mean?"

"That's Greg. Skip over the small talk, why don't you?" Petra said.

"I don't know. Maybe something... Something in... I'm not sure yet."

Greg nodded, his attention straying towards the sound of a television from another room.

"How is your thesis on Beckett?" Kate said, hoping she had remembered it right.

"Coming along. Coming along," he said.

"That's what you've been saying for the last five years," Petra said, taking a spoonful more of the green curry.

"You haven't been here five years. So how can you say that!"

"Other people have told me."

"So, what's this? I get gossiped about in my own house?"

After the meal Kate offered to help with the washing-up. Petra shooed her out.

"Greg does everything on a Wednesday night," she said.

"I'll be off, then. I hope everything goes all right on your travels!"

"Thanks. I'll email you. Let you know. You will look after my stuff? In the wardrobe and chest of drawers? They're locked but..."

"Course I will."

"When I get back maybe there'll be another room here for

you. If not I know a few people in other houses who might be able to help."

Kate left the house and made her way back to Archway tube station. She heard a beep from her phone and it made her instantly apprehensive. Stevie Bussell had her number and she no intention of answering if it was him. She had considered, late last night, whether or not to get rid of the phone and buy another. It would eat into her money though and so she'd dismissed the idea.

She looked down at the screen and relaxed. It was a text from Lucy Bussell.

Lovely to meet you yesterday Kate. Don't forget to write me a letter xxx

She couldn't help but smile. Lucy had no idea that her brother had been rifling through her belongings, looking at her phone, interfering in her life. She was blithely unaware of the way Stevie had confronted Kate yesterday, waving Kate's personal letter to Lucy in her face.

But she had no intention of telling her. Why upset her? She'd done nothing wrong. She sent a short reply to the text and then headed down into the tube station.

TWENTY-NINE

Early the next morning Kate got dressed and ready for work. She'd slept on and off throughout the night but felt tired, the corners of her eyes gritty and her mouth dry.

The room seemed even smaller now she knew she was leaving it. Three or four steps took her from one wall to another. It had become untidier as well. Her rucksack and bag were taking up all the space down one side of the bed. On the other side was a chair with a towel draped over it and pairs of shoes that she she'd left on the floor. She kicked one of them out of her way. Then she went downstairs for breakfast. She picked at some cereal and a plate of toast. The other people in the breakfast room were focused on their newspapers or talking on their phones. After she'd finished she walked over to a large bay window and peered along the pavement as far as she could in either direction.

There was no sign of Stevie Bussell.

She went up to her room and picked up her things for work.

She headed towards the tube station. She found herself breathing normally, her shoulders relaxing, her jaw softening. She was overreacting. She'd faced up to Stevie Bussell and he did not know her new identity; neither did he have any idea where she had been staying. In a couple of days she would be living in Archway out of his reach. She stopped at the crossing and waited for the lights to go green.

A hand rested on her arm.

She looked round instantly, fearful. But it wasn't Stevie Bussell, it was a man in a suit. She frowned at him, glancing down to the ground as though she might have dropped something and he had stopped her to let her know.

"Jennifer?"

He said the word in a whisper, his voice dropping below the noise of the traffic. It was so low she could have sworn that she'd lipread it. She recognised him then. She'd knocked into him after her confrontation with Stevie Bussell. His papers had scattered over the pavement. "Jennifer Jones? I'm Matt Murray. I work for a press agency and I need to talk to you urgently about a story I have concerning you."

She walked off, gripping the edges of her bag. She went as fast as possible but she could hear him calling her, causing other people to turn around and look in her direction.

She stopped and turned to remonstrate with him.

There was a flash which startled her and she saw a man with a camera walking up behind him, taking one picture after another, the sound of the shutter clicking rapidly.

"Jennifer, we have pictures of you talking to Lucy Bussell."

She went to speak but couldn't. She turned away from the camera and tried to walk on but her steps had slowed. They had *pictures*. She thought of Lucy sitting innocently in the café in Finsbury Park, all forgiving, chatting lightly about Donny and her college course and all the while a photographer was crouched somewhere taking photographs. Lucy would be bewildered. A slight girl, she always seemed to be on the edge of things. She didn't cause any trouble; she just attracted it. Kate felt anguish at the thought of her being the centre of attention again when Kate had only ever wanted to say sorry to her.

"Jennifer, my car is round the corner. Come and sit in it for five minutes. I have a proposal for you."

"Was it Stevie Bussell? Did he contact you?"

"He was concerned that you'd written to his sister."

Matt Murray pulled her letter out of his pocket. She recognised the envelope, her own handwriting, the rough tear across the top. Stevie had given the letter to the photographer. Now they had her words as well as her picture. She groaned.

"This needn't be as bad as you think it is."

"Are you paying Stevie for this?"

"Come now, Jennifer. Mr Bussell is a young man on the brink of getting married. He has expenses. We respect that."

The photographer had moved to her side and taken another picture. Several people were staring across the road.

"Tell him to stop that," she said, her voice cracking, her head buzzing with the noise of the traffic.

"Come and sit in the car. Just for five minutes. Let's discuss it."

The reporter was good-looking and his suit was smart. He was holding a set of car keys. The photographer, in contrast, was in jeans and a wrinkled T-shirt. He had a cap on and sunglasses. Although his camera was pointed at her he wasn't looking at *her*, he was fiddling with the buttons and turning it from landscape to portrait and then back again. She wondered if, under the cap, he had hair or was bald like Mr Cottis.

"Come on, Jennifer. Then we can avoid people looking at you."

Matt Murray's voice was like honey; like he was her friend and had her best interests at heart. She stood, frozen, every cell of her body rigid. She suddenly understood that this was the end. She was not going to go and live in the house at Archway in Petra's room. The plastic boxes she'd left there would collect dust. She was never going to use the name *Becky Andrews*. Her dream of shaking off the ties of her release, her probation officer, the police, the string of people who knew her story and who controlled her life, was over. She would be arrested for breaking the law. She would go back to prison and when it was time for her to come out again the whole thing would start over.

She would never be free of it.

"Jennifer, you coming?"

"No," she said, standing firm.

"Think carefully, Jennifer. This stuff will be all over the papers today. If you come with us you can give your side of the story."

To put your side of the story. Hadn't Sara Wright said that very thing to her just two years before?

"I'm not going anywhere with you," she said.

"Jennifer, there's no point in running away. I got your new name from the landlady of the B&B, *Rebecca Andrews*. You can't disappear again…"

She waved him away. She cut through the traffic and headed for the tube station. When she got there she walked along the tunnel and then paused. She leaned against the tiled wall, a feeling of grief gripping at her insides. People filed past her deep in conversation, oblivious to her. No one knew that she was a girl adrift in dangerous waters. The news would emerge later in the day, Matt Murray said, and then it would be in the papers the next day and be read by everyone in her life; that long list of people who had come into contact with her over the years. Added to that were the people she knew in Exmouth; her housemates, the students on her course, the people at the tourist information office. Jimmy Fuller would know; he would also find out how she'd intended to use the name *Rebecca Andrews*. Maybe he would look through his ex-girlfriend's papers and find that her passport was missing. She pictured him sitting cross-legged on the floor of his bedroom, his back against the box holding the file that said *Rebecca Andrews Papers* and realise that Kate had crept out of his bed and stolen it from him.

"Are you all right, dear?" a woman said, looking concerned.

"Thank you, I'm fine," she muttered.

Kate went further into the station. In the concourse she stood in front of a London Underground map and stared at it. There were hundreds of stations in London, the many different coloured lines criss-crossing each other making the city look like a blueprint rather a place. It was another world to her. Her eye moved along some of the lines, some of the stations familiar; Euston, Camden Town, Oxford Street, Marble Arch. Most of the others she'd never heard of; Caledonian Road, Great Portland Street, Seven Sisters, Walthamstow. That was why she wanted to come here, to lose herself in the middle of eight million people. London was like a heaving mass; she'd tried to fit in, to find somewhere to stay and a job.

But her past had followed her like a sad-eyed dog that she'd tried to abandon.

She ran her finger along one of the lines and stopped on a station.

Angel.

An image came into her head; a graveyard, a white alabaster angel, her face still and sad, her hands joined together in prayer. She'd thought of this before. She was familiar with this place. It was printed on a card that she'd been given. She patted the pockets of her rucksack, opening each one, feeling inside it then fastening it again. She finally found the card and looked at the name and address on it. *Angel* was the right station. She traced the line back to Finsbury Park, where she was now. It meant a change of line but it was only a couple of stops.

She got a ticket. In less than fifteen minutes she was above ground, standing in front of Angel station. The pavement was as wide as a street and had a newspaper and magazine stand as well as a mobile coffee van and a flower stall. She stood with her back to the traffic and rang the number on the card. The call went to voicemail so she left a message, her voice strong against the backdrop of traffic and passers-by.

This message is for Sara Wright. This is Kate Rickman. I am in London and I am in trouble. You said if I ever needed your help to get in touch. I need your help now. It's 10:10. I'm standing in front of the Angel tube station and I'll stay here for an hour. Please, when you get this message call me.

She put her phone away and stood to the side of the flower stall. The scent of blooms wafted by her as she leaned against the steel and glass wall of the station. She would wait for an hour. After that she would go to the nearest police station and hand herself in.

Twenty minutes later a car pulled up, its hazard lights flashing on and off.

Kate stared at it, holding her breath. The driver's door opened and Sara Wright stood there. Kate felt her legs wobble with relief as she walked towards the journalist and got into the passenger seat of her car.

THIRTY

Kate was in a meeting room at the television centre where Sara Wright worked. There was a round table with chairs for ten people. In the middle of it sat an arrangement of flowers, pale pink roses and carnations. On the wall opposite was a line of clocks which showed the time in different parts of the world; London, New York, Moscow, Johannesburg, Beijing. The other side of the room was glass which looked down onto the road outside. She was seven storeys up. She could see traffic but the sound was far away. From here it reminded her of the sound of the surf. She closed her eyes for a few moments and leaned her forehead against the cool glass. She saw herself on the beach at Exmouth, striding along the water's edge, her walking boots digging deep into the packed sand, the waves crashing further out, the sea racing towards her ankles.

Now she felt thick carpet under her feet. On the table, in front of her, were a packet of sandwiches and a large cardboard cup of coffee. She'd drunk the coffee but not touched the food. She sat down again and her hand played with the sides of the lukewarm cup and she wondered where everyone had got to.

Earlier there had been a meeting with Sara's boss, Mr Cosgrove. He was a tall thin man with steel-grey hair and half-moon glasses. He seemed to have a permanent frown, his forehead in lines. He had been polite but not friendly. Sara had spent some time explaining the situation, checking with Kate now and then if what she was saying was right. Kate agreed, looking at the editor for some kind of eye contact or softening of attitude. He focused on Sara though and made notes on an A4 pad. After a while he left and Sara told her to give him some time. *He needs to think it all through*, *there are legal implications*, she said. Then she left, making sure that Kate had everything she needed.

Kate's bags were leaning against one of the table legs. Sara had dropped Kate off at the offices of the television company and then driven to the B&B and packed Kate's belongings and paid her bill.

She reached into her rucksack and felt about for her old phone. Now she could turn it on because her whereabouts would be known anyway. In a couple of hours, when the afternoon newspaper came out in London, the story would be public. Then she might get a call from Julia Masters demanding to know what was going on. There might be other calls as well. She switched her mobile on and watched as it came to life. There were a number of beeps indicating missed calls or texts. She looked at the screen. There were seven missed calls; two from Sally and five from Jimmy. There were also six texts; one from Sally, one from Aimee and four from Jimmy.

The missed calls were on Sunday and Monday. The texts were from the day before, Wednesday.

She opened Sally's.

> *Hi Kate. I'm guessing you met up with your pals in Taunton. Give me a call or send me a text so that I know you're OK!!!!*

Next she looked at Aimee's.

> *Hope your camping trip is going well. Don't forget to call in when you come back. Luv Aimee* ☺

Then she looked at Jimmy's. The first was Wednesday, 6:02am.

> *Woke up early and thinking about you. Call me xxxxx*

The second was sent at 12:59pm.

> *When you come back you can make me some bread! xxxxx*

The third was late the previous evening, 11:32pm.

> *I'm guessing you've no reception out on the moors. Did I tell you how much I like you? And it's not because you remind me of my ex-girlfriend. I'm counting the days till you come back xxxxx*

She turned it off. Soon not just Jimmy but everybody she knew in Exmouth would know about her. Sara had explained to her how it worked. Matt Murray was employed by a news agency. He'd collected the details of her story plus photographic evidence. These things would be in the London *Evening Standard*. Then the story would be picked up by the television news stations and the following morning it would be in the daily papers. Matt Murray would keep some stuff back, perhaps the photographs of the meeting with Lucy Bussell and the letter, so that he could sell the story over again to one of the tabloids.

It might be on the evening news or at the very least it would be picked up by local news stations. The address on Kate's letter was in Exmouth so the local news stations there would cover it. She pictured Sally eating a sandwich at the kitchen table, half an eye on the small television in the corner. Ruth might be making some food for her and Robbie and would look up when the name *Kate Rickman* was mentioned.

Jimmy might not find out straight away because he spent a lot of time in his room listening to music or watching DVDs, but maybe there would be a knock on his door and one of the guys would say, *That girl you're seeing, her name's Kate Rickman, right? Only there's something on the news…*

The door of the room opened and Mr Cosgrove came in, looking harassed. Sara Wright followed him. From behind him she gave Kate a thumbs-up sign. Kate knew she ought to feel relieved and yet inside there was a sense of dread about what she was going to do.

"Now," Mr Cosgrove said, looking down at the piece of paper in his hand. "We have fixed a press conference for one o'clock. It will take place in one of our news studios and it will consist of you reading a statement and taking some questions from the press. At present we have sent out a fairly innocuous description of this conference. We have said that it concerns *Conditions of Parole for Ex-Offenders.*"

He paused and glanced at Kate. He took his glasses off and rubbed the bridge of his nose. His eyes seemed to sink back into his head and he looked like he needed a good night's sleep.

"This will attract the more academic sections of the press, those particularly interested in the issue of prison reform and so on. It implies the results of some study or other so no one will be expecting you to speak. When you do read your statement it will cause some surprise and the journalists there will immediately contact their newspapers with what will be seen as a scoop. The news will filter out and there will be huge interest in the story. We will, of course, broadcast an interview with you in all our bulletins during the rest of the day and this evening."

Kate nodded. She glanced at the *London* clock on the wall. It was 12:20.

"This may have the effect of scuppering the news agency story or it may not. I don't think that will concern you. There are, however, some things that you need to be ready for. Firstly, the press will say that you only went public because you know that the newspapers already had a story."

"That's true. I can't argue with it," Kate said.

"Secondly, there may be sections of the press who argue that this is a publicity stunt to enable Sara Wright to sell her book. Indeed, this was something I had to consider very strongly when I was approached by Sara. There may be suggestions that you are benefitting financially from this 'exposé'."

Kate didn't speak. It was something she hadn't considered.

"And thirdly," he went on, "this press conference, the interview you are going to do, this will bring people out of the woodwork. There may be people from your past who will decide they want contact with you. The dead girl's parents, for example."

Kate slumped back in the chair. Mr and Mrs Livingstone. Could she face them, if she had to?

"There is still the opportunity to get in touch with your probation officer and explain what has happened. You may have to present yourself at a police station and I'm sure Sara will go with you and give you advice. You'll be reprimanded and moved and start your life again with another identity. There is no need for you to go public if you don't want to."

To start again with a new name, a new history. Looking over her shoulder, waiting for a detective or a journalist or a local policeman to knock at her door and drag her through everything again. She couldn't do it any more. She shook her head.

"And," Sara said, "your mother may want to see you."

Kate looked down at her hands. Her fingers were woven tightly. Her knuckles were white.

"Can I stop my mother from seeing me? Am I allowed to do that?"

"If she refused to leave you alone, you'd have to make a case for it, in front of a judge. Maybe get a restraining order."

"Are you absolutely sure about this? Kate?" Mr Cosgrove said, his eyes searching her face.

"Yes, I am," she said.

The news studio had three people sitting in the audience as Kate entered, walking between Mr Cosgrove and Sara. It was a small area with a long table down one end and rows of chairs filling the rest of the room. The table had four seats behind it and microphones at each place. There were no windows but bright lights which made it feel muggy and warm. Sara placed a chair in front of the door to keep it open.

When they sat behind the table Kate suddenly felt panicky. In front of her was the statement that she and Sara had written. It was in her handwriting, like the letter she had sent to Lucy. That had been weeks before. Back then she'd thought that that was the extent of what she would do. An apology to a girl who she had treated badly; but then there was the other girl who she had treated much worse. There was no apology that she could make to Michelle Livingstone. She stared down at the page in front of her and saw that her hands were trembling. How long would this take? Longer than she wanted.

Looking up she saw that there were now five people in the audience. Just then several other people came into the room, all talking to each other, one or two laughing. They sidled along a row and one or two of them looked curiously at Kate.

"Is this everybody?" Kate whispered to Sara.

"This is a good number for a low-key press conference," Sara said, her face turned to Kate's ear. "Remember, it's not these people who are so important. This will be broadcast on the twenty-four-hour news stream."

A few moments later an elderly woman rushed in, apologising. She sat down and proceeded to take a sandwich from a packet and eat it hungrily.

"Prison rights campaigner. Freelance journalist," Sara said quietly.

Mr Cosgrove started to speak. His voice sounded very loud in the small space.

"You all know, me, James Cosgrove, Commissioning Editor. This press conference has been called at short notice. Indeed, I only knew about it myself an hour or so ago. It is, however, an important briefing, for reasons that you will see. The announcement here could have a bearing on the debate regarding the treatment of ex-offenders. For that reason I would like to introduce Jennifer Jones, who has a statement to read out, and then will take questions."

A couple of people looked up and directed their gaze to Kate. The prison rights campaigner stopped chewing.

"You can start now," Mr Cosgrove said.

Kate cleared her throat.

"My name is..." she began.

The level of her voice was loud, too loud; people would probably hear it all through the building. She moved her head back from the microphone and started again, her voice running swiftly through the words in front of her, hardly taking a breath.

"My name is Jennifer Jones and I would like to read you a short statement. Eight years ago I killed a girl called Michelle Livingstone and I was sent to a secure unit. Two years and nine months ago I was released and given a new identity. I lived in Croydon for nine months but had to move again and for the past two years I have been living in Devon and have been a student at Exeter University under the name of Kate Rickman."

She paused and looked round. Most of the audience were staring at her. Some were sitting up straight, their faces rapt, not quite sure of what they had stumbled on. A couple of the men immediately began to tap at their phones. Kate went on, her voice quavering, sounding high.

"Some weeks ago I sent a letter to Lucy Bussell, the third girl who was involved in the events of that day. I sent this letter to apologise and I knew as I was doing it that it was going against the terms of my release. A few days ago I left the place I lived in Devon and took a train to London in order to start a new life on my own without the knowledge of the authorities. I was wrong to do that and shall bear the consequences of that action over the coming days."

There wasn't a sound in the room. Every face was fixed on Kate's.

"My reason for giving this press conference is that I now intend to live my life with my birth name, Jennifer Jones. I am no longer prepared to live a lie. If this means I have to stay in prison then so be it. I hope that in time the authorities and the public will allow me to live normally."

She looked around for any appalled expressions. She went on to say her last line. She started to speak but found she couldn't. She picked up a glass and drank some water. Then she looked around, making eye contact with as many in the audience as she could.

"However I end up living, no matter how my life turns out, I will never forget nor forgive myself for what happened to Michelle Livingstone."

She sat back. There was a moment's silence. It sounded

comforting, like being underwater. Then the voices exploded as the questions started. Mr Cosgrove stood up.

"One question at a time, please. One at a time."

Kate was sitting in a coffee bar at Paddington Station with Sara Wright. She was to catch the 4.20 train to Exeter. She'd spent the afternoon doing an interview for the evening news shows. The televised interview would last about ten minutes but the filming seemed to have taken forever.

While she was waiting she composed a text to Lucy Bussell.

Dear Lucy, you will see things in the press about me today. Don't be upset. It's nothing for you to worry about. The one good thing about coming to London was meeting you. Hope you and Donny are OK. I will write again if I'm allowed xxxxx

She sent the message.

"You all right?" Sara said.

"Fine."

"Time to go? Got your ticket?"

Kate showed the ticket. She followed Sara towards the ticket gates.

"Not nervous about going back?"

"Not really. I've got to get it over with. Face people."

"Don't forget to look out for Don Jordan. He said he'd wait just outside the station for you. He's done a lot of legal aid work in Exeter so he'll make sure everything's done properly."

Mr Cosgrove had arranged for a local solicitor to meet Kate

and take her to the police station so that she could hand herself in. It was a relief that it was out of her hands now.

"I'd better go," she said.

"Look after yourself," Sara said. "Maybe this will all be for the best."

"I know one thing," Kate said. "Your book will sell more copies."

Sara nodded and shrugged at the same time. Kate slipped her ticket into the machine and went through the gates. She didn't look back.

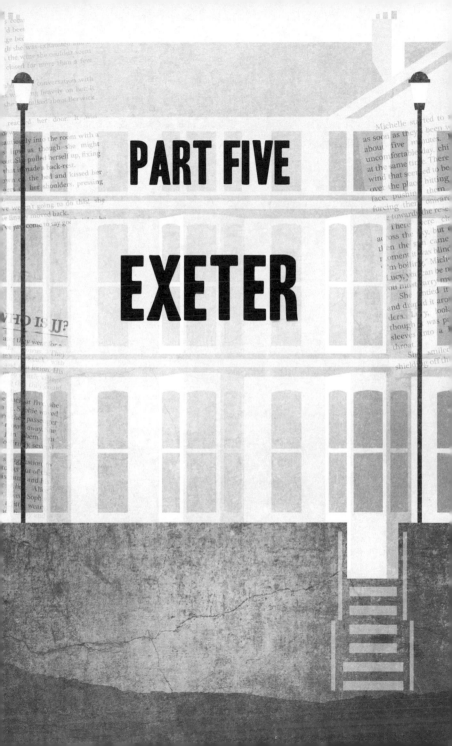

PART FIVE

EXETER

THIRTY-ONE

Jennifer sat on the train, slumped against the window. She was tired. The carriage she was in was half empty and she stared out onto the passing countryside as the train sped through. She'd deliberately turned her phone off and put it into her bag. After the stress of the morning and the time it took to do the interview she didn't want any actual contact with anyone. There would be plenty of that once she got to Exeter.

Her mother crept into her thoughts, though.

The press would contact Carol Jones asking for her opinion on the latest developments. Carol Jones, the model, would be keen to get involved. *Will you be sending a photographer?* she might say and begin to sort out her clothes and apply her make-up. No doubt she would hold up her outfits so that her new husband would look them over and decide which showed her in the most flattering light.

Would she, for whatever reason of her own, jump in a car and come down to Exmouth and try and see her daughter? Jennifer hoped she wouldn't. She had no interest in Carol Jones. It was some years since she'd had any contact with her at all. The last time had been when she was in detention. During a visit her mother had taken a photograph of her sitting on a bench in the grounds. Days later she'd sold that photograph to a tabloid newspaper and Jennifer had stopped any contact between them. Photographs were a kind of currency for Carol Jones – she paid for things with them or she was rewarded with them for doing some sort of dirty work. Her life was one long reel of film. Somewhere along it, Jennifer had faded out.

She'd glimpsed her mother for the last time two years before when her life in Croydon had ended. Carol Jones had been on her way then to stage a meeting with Jennifer but Jennifer had been spirited away so the meeting had not happened.

Would she be able to avoid such a meeting now?

It was one of the problems she would have to face.

She thought about the interview that she'd done. She'd had to have make-up put on by a girl who looked about her age and who had chatted about her boyfriend who had asked her to move in with him. She'd stared at her face in the mirror as foundation had been applied, and blusher and lipstick. It had seemed bizarre and strange to be treated like a celebrity.

Another journalist, an older woman, Jane Curran, had taken the interview. Her questions had been sympathetic but then, at the end of the interview, out of the blue, she'd said, *And how do you expect the parents of the dead girl to react to this media circus that has exploded?* She had stumbled over her answer, saying that she hadn't wanted it to be like this, but Jane Curran had simply looked her in the eye and said, *If you'd stayed where you were, Miss Jones, none of this would have happened. Many prisoners are released with new identities to protect them from reprisals. Why was it so difficult for you to live with it?*

250

She stumbled out her answers and then, all of a sudden, it was finished and she could go.

The train was due into Exmouth Central just before seven. As it began to slow she walked along the carriage with her bags. Further up, near the front, in a seat where someone had been sitting until a couple of stops before, was a copy of the London *Evening Standard*. She looked at the front page. There was an article about a football player at the top but the bottom half of the page had her story. *Jennifer Jones in London: Child Killer Attempts Contact with Third Girl*. Underneath, at the side of the article was a photo of her taken that morning, on the pavement across the road from Finsbury Park station. She looked at it for a few moments, her mouth hard and straight. She was public property: it was something she would have to get used to.

She got off the train and headed for the ticket barriers. Just beyond them she could see a small man with straggly hair standing looking quizzically at the travellers. She put her hand up and he smiled.

"Jennifer Jones?" he said, when she got up to him.

She nodded. Her real name felt odd now, as if *it* belonged to someone else and she was borrowing it. He began to walk and speak at the same time.

"I'm Don Jordan. My car's close by. I've spoken at length with Sara Wright and she's filled me in on your situation. I've been in touch with the police and informed them that you intend to present yourself voluntarily at the Exeter station, in effect to *hand yourself in*. What they intend to do with you, well, we'll have to wait and see."

He was in a hurry. He was wearing dark trousers and a short-sleeved shirt. On his belt at the side was a holder for his mobile phone and he reached for it as she followed him towards the car park. He took a call briefly and then placed it back, fastening the top flap so it was hidden away.

"This is my wife's car so it's a bit of a mess."

Jennifer put her bags into the back seat to the side of a child's car seat. There were a couple of rattles lying in the footwell.

"I've also been in touch with Julia Masters, your probation officer. She will try to get to the police station this evening after her appointments. Is there anything you'd like to ask me?"

He was leaning across the steering wheel looking to one side and then to the other, checking the traffic. The car pulled out and Jennifer asked him the question that had been playing around her head ever since the press conference.

"Will they send me back to prison?"

"Hard to say," he said, without a moment's thought. "My guess is that there'll be a hearing in the morning, probably in front of a magistrate. You have certainly transgressed some of the agreed boundaries and of course you've come out publicly, which won't please the authorities. We'll have to see."

Jennifer sat very still.

"I'll come into the station with you and we will see how the police deal with your case. There's a possibility you may be bailed, cautioned, told to report back to the station in the morning. Or they may want you to stay overnight until the hearing tomorrow – that's if it is tomorrow. It all depends who is in charge. We shall see."

They parked along the road from the police station. Jennifer picked her bags out of the back of the car and walked with heavy legs towards the front entrance. The last time she had been here was when they'd taken her in for questioning about the Jodie Mills murder. Then she had come in a car and been ushered into the station from a back entrance. Now they had to press an intercom button and Don Jordan spoke succinctly into the mouthpiece and the doors swung open. Jennifer walked behind the solicitor, ignoring the half a dozen people who were sitting in the waiting area. When they got to the counter she let her rucksack slide off her arm and onto the floor and placed her other bag by its side. A uniformed officer came towards them. Don Jordan spoke immediately, his voice booming out with authority.

"I am Donald Jordan and I'm here to represent my client, Jennifer Jones. I called earlier to outline my intentions. Jennifer Jones is voluntarily attending the station as recent events have led her to break the conditions of her release two years and nine months ago."

The officer nodded. He picked up a telephone and made a call. Don Jordan stood to attention as though there was no awkwardness in the situation. The officer appeared to be speaking to someone but his words were muffled and Jennifer couldn't make out what was being said. Don Jordan's phone beeped and he flipped open the pouch and pulled it out. Kate heard the name *Julia* and thought that it was probably her probation officer. *OK!* Don Jordan said, jauntily. *OK! I'll tell Jennifer.*

"Your probation officer has been held up. She will be here later," he said, holding onto his phone for a moment before replacing it in its holder.

The officer finished his call. "Someone will be along to deal with you. Take a seat. I'm not sure how long they will be."

They sat down. Jennifer prepared herself for a long wait. The inner door opened suddenly though and a couple of officers came out, talking, one of them laughing at something the other one had said. Just behind them was a plain-clothes officer, a detective. Jennifer recognised him immediately. DC Simon Kelsey. Her heart sank. He spoke to the officer on the desk who nodded in their direction, then he said something to the other officer who grinned. Then he walked towards them. Don Jordan stood up.

"I'm DC Simon Kelsey, Mr Jordan. Perhaps you and your client would care to come with me."

He couldn't even say her name. She watched his back as he pressed an entry buzzer. His shoulders seemed to ripple; perhaps with pleasure.

THIRTY-TWO

She was taken to a cell. It was ten o'clock and she'd been assured that the hearing would take place the following morning and Don Jordan would apply for – and get – bail. A further hearing would have to be scheduled, Don Jordan was positive. *You've not committed any crime. You've annoyed the probation service and the parole authorities won't like the fact that you're choosing to live under your own name. But you've served your sentence.*

Tonight, though, she had to stay in police custody.

She'd been taken there by DC Simon Kelsey and he had waited in the corridor until the door was locked by the custody sergeant. Even then she had sensed him standing outside the door, listening to see if she would shout or cry out. Instead she sat rigid, her face turned away, staring at the wall opposite the door. There was no window, just rows of glass bricks near the top where light shone through. Eventually she heard him walk away, his footsteps receding.

The cell was small and heavy with the smell of disinfectant. She sat on the bed, a thin blanket pooled at her ankles. She wouldn't sleep, she *couldn't* sleep. She thought about the news reports and wondered who had seen them and what their reaction had been. Mainly she thought about Jimmy Fuller, who might think that the only reason she had been with him was so that she could steal his ex-girlfriend's passport. Jimmy's heart was already bruised, the girl he had loved working on a dig in Scotland, instead of living in a house in Exmouth with him. Now his rebound girlfriend had proved false in many more ways than one.

There was some noise out in the corridor, a female voice, talking to the sergeant. The door rattled and then it opened and Julia Masters was standing there. In her hand she had a bottle of water and a packet of sandwiches. The custody sergeant was holding a chair. He placed it in the cell.

"You're allowed to eat this while I'm here," Julia said, handing the food to her.

"Thank you," Jennifer said.

She peeled back the wrapper, took a sandwich out and bit a corner of it off. She hadn't realised that she was hungry. Julia was making herself comfortable, placing her bag on one side of her chair and her briefcase on the other.

"I had some appointments. Then I had to go home and wait for my husband to get home from work so that he could sit with Justin and Peter."

"Sorry to cause you so much trouble."

"Are you, Kate?"

Julia looked pointedly at her.

"It's *Jennifer* now."

Julia let out a sigh. She looked tired. Her hair was pulled back with a tie and she had no earrings on.

"Do you really think that reverting to your birth name will

make your life any better?" she said. "It won't. It will make it a lot worse. Everyone will know what you've done! Is that what you want? To go through your life with people staring at you, pointing fingers at you? *That's the girl who killed the ten-year-old.*"

"I was ten years old myself."

"You don't need to tell me. I know everything about your case. Every single thing!"

"I'm tired of living a lie."

"Maybe you'll feel differently in a few weeks' time."

"Why are you so angry at me?"

"Because of the trouble we went to hide your identity. Arrangements had to be made, people's time was taken up. Public money was spent on you, Kate!"

"Have you just come here to shout at me?"

"No. No." Julia looked sheepish. "Course not. I guess it's just late and I'm tired. I came to tell you that I'll be there at the hearing in the morning and I'll be speaking on your behalf."

"Thank you."

"But you know that it won't make any difference to your commitments to me. You'll still have your appointments with me whatever your name is."

"I know."

"I just wanted you to know that you have my support."

"Do I?"

Julia stared at Jennifer, her mouth open, an expression of exasperation on her face.

"You've never liked me, have you?" she said.

Jennifer was taken aback. It might well have been true and

maybe they both knew it, but it was an awkward thing to say out loud. She didn't know how to answer.

"I had such good reports about you from your other probation officers. *A bright girl, a terrific student. A person who wants to do what is right. She is a delight to work with. Just be careful that she doesn't crumple under pressure.* But I never found that person. All I found was a stroppy teenage girl who thought she'd been dealt a bad hand. I've tried to help you as much as I could, but you didn't go out of your way to make it easy."

"I'm sorry," she said. "I just tried to keep myself to myself."

"Standoffish I could have handled, but at times you've been like a snappy dog."

Jennifer felt herself slump. She put the half-finished sandwich back into the packet.

"I've been close to people before. My first probation officer, Jill. She was great. She looked after me whatever happened. The woman I lived with in Croydon, Rosie. She… She was like a mother to me. I had to leave her and Jill behind though. That was hard. I missed them. I missed Rosie every day. It was like I was grieving for her. I just thought it was better not to get close to people again."

Julia blew through her teeth.

"I didn't want to take anyone's place. I just didn't want to feel that you weren't always at odds with me."

"I'll try to be different."

"Maybe you will," she said, softly. "Finish your sandwich. Then I'll go."

Jennifer ate the sandwich and drank the water. When Julia got up to leave she remembered something.

"Where will I live? After the hearing?"

"Where you're living now!" Julia said.

"But Sally and Ruth might not feel comfortable about my past...."

"They've always known! Why do you think they took you in? I told them right at the beginning."

"Thank you," she whispered.

"OK, *Jennifer*. Let's hope tomorrow and what comes after is what you wanted."

Later, long after Julia had gone home, she lay down on the bed. Sally and Ruth had never given any hint that they'd known. And Julia had arranged it all. Why had she always been so harsh on her? It was a question she couldn't quite answer.

She dozed for a while then woke up with a start. It was 01:06. She listened for sounds of other prisoners but there didn't seem to be any. It was Thursday night and not much crime, perhaps.

She thought about Jodie Mills, murdered by a man who worked at Sandy Bay as a gardener in the caravan parks. Had he sat here, in this very cell? It made her shiver a little, and yet what was the difference between her and that man? He had taken a girl's life, but *so had she*. Did that make her the same as him?

She shook her head. She was not the same, *she was not*. She turned her face into the pillow. Too much death.

She remembered Joe Bussell who had gone to a DIY store and bought wire cutters and rope. He'd queued up like everyone else and paid maybe with cash or a card. Then he'd carried his purchases in a bag and hanged himself at the back of Kings Cross station.

Mr Cottis came into her mind. Mr Cottis always seemed to

be somewhere at the edge of her thoughts, a recurring ghost. Joe Bussell had been doing some kind of apprenticeship with him. He'd been coping really well, Lucy had said, and then for no reason he had killed himself. Jennifer wondered what his days with Mr Cottis were like; photographing family portraits? Wedding photos?

Or were they taking other kinds of pictures entirely?

Jennifer closed her eyes tightly. She tried to sleep. Maybe, for a while she did.

When she opened her eyes there was light coming through the glass bricks. She looked at the clock on the wall. It was 05:07am. She got off the bed and stretched her legs. She bent down at the sink and splashed her face. Then she went to the door and knocked. Moments later an officer came along. He looked wary, as if he expected her to try and escape.

"I'd like to talk with DI Lauren Heart," Jennifer said.

"I don't know whether she's in or not. I can get someone else."

"No, it's just her I just need to speak to."

The officer went off grumbling. Jennifer sat back down. It was achingly early and unless Lauren Heart was on a night shift she'd probably be at home with her family. It would be hours before she could speak to her, if at all. In fact, it was barely an hour later that the door was opened and Lauren Heart stood there. Jennifer sat up, her head a little dazed because she had dropped off to sleep again. She crossed her arms and tried to look straight at the detective. The last time they'd spoke DI Heart had told Jennifer (Kate, then) a few bald truths and it had not been easy for her to listen to them. Now the detective looked tired. The uniformed officer followed her in with a chair for her to sit on.

"Will you have some tea, ma'am?" he said.

"Sure. Milk, no sugar. Jennifer? Will you have tea?"

"Yes, black, please."

The door was left open. Lauren Heart pushed the fingers of one hand through her hair. Then she yawned and covered her mouth with her free hand.

"What do you want, Jennifer?" she said, softly.

"I have some information that I maybe should have told the police about years ago but I never did."

"Regarding your case? The killing of Michelle Livingstone?"

"No, not really."

The custody sergeant came into the room holding two cups and saucers. He passed one to DI Heart and the other to Jennifer. Steam rolled off the top of Jennifer's.

"Anything else, ma'am?"

"No, thank you."

DI Heart looked quizzically at Jennifer. "What do you want to tell me? I thought you'd done all your talking on the television, yesterday."

Jennifer gulped at the boiling tea. What had she expected? A sympathetic response from the detective? Gratitude? DI Heart had been quite clear that she owed Jennifer Jones nothing. She stared at DI Heart's hand. She was wearing the garnet ring that looked too big. Maybe it was something she never took off. Jennifer wanted to ask her about it but it gave her a bad feeling; as if the ring was a memento of something sad. Under the strip light it glowed, a deep blood red.

"When I was ten and I lived with my mother in Berwick

she had an agent, a man who took her photos. His name was Mr Cottis, Kenneth Cottis. He was friends with the Bussell family and I guess that's how my mother met him. He was around the house a lot in those days and one day he asked if he could photograph me."

DI Heart sipped at her tea. Jennifer faltered. Was there really much to tell?

"I felt at the time – I was only ten, of course – I felt that what he was asking was not right. He gave me old-fashioned school clothes to dress up in and I was sure that something was wrong with what he was asking me to do."

"Did he touch you? Did he take photographs of you? What are you getting at?"

DI Heart put her cup on the floor. She leaned forward, her hands clasped.

Now Jennifer had to lie.

"No. I never posed for him, but he had a suitcase that held his photos and I was nosing around in it one day and I saw some pictures of…" She paused, remembering the day, the naked photos she saw of her mother; the sight that had filled her with confusion.

"Children? Pornographic photos?"

"Yes, children. I think so. I might have been wrong. I was only ten. I might not have understood what I was looking at."

It was a small lie but it told a bigger truth.

DI Heart's face had darkened.

"And where is this man now?"

"He has a photography business in Alexandra Palace, north London. I saw it advertised on the internet."

"This certainly made an impression on you. You were ten,

you say? Was it round about the time of Michelle's death?"

"Sometime round then."

"Did your mother know about this?"

Jennifer looked at DI Heart. She felt her face tremble.

"Did she know, Jennifer?"

"No." She shook her head, affronted. "I never told her. If my mother had known she would have gone to the police. She would *never* have let such a thing happen to me. She never knew. She *loved* me. I kept it from her."

DI Lauren Heart sat back.

"My mother loved me. She did," Jennifer whispered, fiercely.

The policewoman touched her ring, making it swivel on her finger. She looked as if she wanted to ask something else, but in the end decided against it.

"Thank you for the information, Jennifer. We shall certainly look into it."

THIRTY-THREE

Jennifer was getting ready to go to a meeting at Exeter University. It was the second time she had attended that week. Her change of name and the accompanying publicity had sent the pastoral staff into panic mode. For a while, it had looked as though she might have to transfer and take the last year of her degree somewhere else. Julia Masters had stepped in, though. She made her view quite clear. The court authorities had allowed Jennifer Jones her continued freedom and so the university had no business undermining that by trying to send her somewhere else.

It seemed that she had yet another reason to be grateful to Julia Masters.

She was running a little late. She was standing at the kitchen table finishing a coffee and some toast and looking over some documents that she'd downloaded and printed off regarding her course. Her bag was sitting neatly on the chair next to her and her phone was flat on the table and she glanced at the screen of it from time to time.

"Busy day?" Sally said, coming into the kitchen.

"A meeting with the pastoral team. I'm also going to try

and catch a couple of my tutors, see if I can have a word with them, before the course officially starts."

"Wow, that sounds like hard work! You students!"

"I do have *studying* to do as well," she said, in a voice of mock outrage. "I let it all drift a bit last year. I want to see if I can retake some things."

"Everything all right? At university?"

"Oh, you know, not everyone's back yet. There've been a few looks from staff, a few people nudging each other when I walk past, but it's a big place. Most people are too interested in themselves to worry about the fact that my name has changed. Most of them won't have even read the story and if they have …" Jennifer shrugged.

Jennifer began to pack the printed document and her phone into her bag. What she had said wasn't quite true. There had been a woman in the course admin office, Rosemary, who had complained about her. Kate had been waiting outside the door for the office to open when she heard the voice, querulous; *I didn't take this job so that I could sit in the same room as a murderer!* Rosemary, a woman who had always been really friendly, had swept past her moments later and walked off up the corridor. Another one of the admin staff had given an apologetic smile and helped her with her course query.

She'd seen some of the girls she had been friendly with the previous year. They'd returned to university early, moving in to new houses. They'd not snubbed her completely, but there had been no invites for lunch or coffee or drinks in the university bar. Jennifer was relieved. She dreaded questions, the inevitable enquiries. *So, what happened? How come? Was it, like, self-defence? If you didn't mean to do it how come you didn't call an ambulance? What was it like in prison?* Being close to people meant that they were entitled to some of your life story; Jennifer was pleased that she had become unpopular.

Sally was beating a couple of eggs in a jug. She was looking a little sleepy, her dressing gown bunched over where it hadn't been tied properly. She yawned, using her forearm to cover her mouth.

"Heard from Jimmy?" she said.

Jennifer shook her head. She picked up her bag. "I'll see you tonight. Remember, I'm cooking. Vegetable casserole. Will Robbie be here?"

"Does the night follow day?"

Jennifer left the house and headed down the hill towards the bus terminal. After a summer of walking to work on the esplanade it felt odd to be taking the bus again. It was sunny but there was a hint of cold in the air. Some gulls were sitting on the roof of a garage looking subdued, as though they knew the summer was over. The bus station was in shadow and she wished she'd worn a jacket. She pulled her phone out of her bag and checked it once more.

The screen was blank. No missed calls, no text messages.

Had she really thought that Jimmy might get in touch?

On the day after the court hearing she'd written him a letter and enclosed the passport she'd taken from his room. She'd tried to explain, in a faltering way, to sum up her life, to describe, to make excuses. In the end she'd deleted her attempts and sent him a few handwritten lines.

Dear Jimmy,

I know you'll think badly of me now that you know the truth. I can't make any excuses. I did what I did. I have to live with that. At least I don't have to pretend any more. I'm enclosing Rebecca's passport. I never actually used it. I'm sorry I took it. I was going through a desperate time.

Jennifer Jones.

She had been tempted to put *Kate* in brackets after her name just to reassure him that she was the same person he'd known but then she thought, *What's the point?* It wasn't like she'd been in love with him. He was a nice lad, easy to spend time with, but like everything else it had been predicated on a lie. Now she had to step out, make her life as Jennifer Jones. Finish her degree, get a job, find a place for herself in this world.

"Well, well, look who it is."

A loud voice broke into her thoughts. She saw Aimee standing a few metres away, with her daughter, Louise. She began to smile but immediately sensed that it wasn't the right thing to do. Aimee was holding her daughter's hand up high, protectively, as though someone might be threatening to rip her away.

"You've got a nerve coming back here," Aimee said, her eyes steely.

Some of the people at the bus stop looked round. Jennifer stepped away from the queue. She made eye contact with Louise, who looked puzzled. Aimee used her free hand to edge her daughter back so that she was standing partially behind her.

"You lied to us, to everyone. When all the while you'd done this terrible thing! There should be a law against people like you, people with fake IDs pretending to be like everyone else. I told you things about my family, my daughter…"

"Mummy, what's wrong?" Louise said.

Aimee took a step towards her, holding her daughter behind her back. Jennifer looked around, embarrassed. She could just walk away, but where would she go? She was on her way to college. She had to expect that some people might react badly. This was something she had to endure. A group of women at the bus stop were staring at them. A schoolgirl, chewing gum, was pulling her earphones out, one by one, so that she could listen.

"Aimee, I…I had to live like that. It wasn't my choice."

"It was your choice to *kill* someone! A child!" she hissed.

A ticket inspector at another bus stop was frowning at them. He probably thought it was just an argument between two women.

"I'm sorry…I don't know what to say…" Her voice dropped to a whisper.

"Why don't you pack your bags and get away from here. We don't want your sort living here."

Jennifer stared down at the ground. She wondered how much longer she would stand there. Aimee was still talking, her voice droning on. *You pretended to be someone else! You lied to me and I gave you my friendship!* Louise was interrupting, asking her mother what was wrong. Her voice sounded high, as though she might burst into tears at any moment. The sound of a bus wheezing to a halt alongside them filled Jennifer's ears and without a word she spun on her heel and walked towards it, ignoring Aimee's tirade. She got on the bus and went up the back. She got a book out of her bag and opened it randomly and stared down at the pages, her eyes blurring on the print. She could hear other people getting onto the bus, the women perhaps who had been watching, the schoolgirl who had found the scene interesting enough to take her earphones out. There were other footsteps as well, and chatter, some boys bursting onto the bus on their way to school. She didn't look up, she just tuned in and out of the fragments of conversation and felt her nerves uncoiling. It was clear that Aimee hadn't followed her onto the bus.

She looked up from her book.

There was a banging on the window beside her. She turned and saw Aimee's furious face, her mouth opening and shutting, as the bus moved away from the terminal and headed out onto the road. She swivelled and looked out the back window and saw Aimee standing still, her daughter next to her, rubbing her eyes as if she was crying.

She pulled a tissue out of her pocket and held it to her mouth, afraid she was going to burst into sobs. After a few moments she calmed down. She started to shred the tissue, pulling it into strips. Then she balled up the mess of tissue and pushed it down the side of her bag. She hugged herself. She was cold. She should definitely have worn a jacket. Or maybe she should have stayed at home, in her room, with the duvet pulled around her.

After the meeting with her mentor – *Things might be difficult for you but we will support you, Jennifer* – she walked towards the refectory at the far end of the campus. It was brimming with students but they were all new, preparing for their fresher's week. She was relaxed because there was no chance of her bumping into anyone she knew. She bought a sandwich and a drink and took it out onto the grass. She sat down cross-legged and ate her sandwich while she stared off into the distance and wondered whether she'd done the right thing coming back to Exmouth. The meeting with Aimee had shaken her.

What had she expected? That everyone would be sweet and understanding? Sally and Ruth had welcomed her back and she had to be grateful for that. Even Robbie, who often didn't seem to know which day of the week it was, had been kind. *We've all got our skeletons*, he'd said mysteriously to her, and she'd looked at him in a new light. His skeletons couldn't have been as real as hers were though.

She had to stay. She had to live there as *Jennifer Jones*, otherwise it had all been a waste of time.

She stood up and took the food packaging to a bin. Then she saw a familiar face. Jimmy Fuller was walking towards her along the paths with some other students. She looked around for somewhere to go, to hide, so that she could avoid a meeting with him but it was too late. He'd seen her.

She patted her top, brushing off crumbs. Would he come across? Speak to her? She braced herself and looked over at him. He gave her a smile and a wave and continued talking to the students who were with him. As if she was someone he knew slightly, an acquaintance. She returned the wave and walked back across the grass towards the block where the library was. She went quickly, trying to put as much distance between them as she could. He was outwardly friendly; she had to be satisfied with that. She thought of Aimee again, her face twisted in hatred. Anything was better than that.

When she got home there was a letter for her. The address was handwritten and the envelope had been franked. She pulled it open and inside there was a web page that had been printed off. It was from a news site, the *Alexandra Palace Online Local*. Most of it seemed to be filled with adverts but down the middle was a piece of news.

> *Raid at Photographer's Yields Child Pornography*
> *Mr Kenneth Cottis was arrested by police after a tip-off from a member of the public. During a search of his property indecent material was found and when his computer and hard drive were examined thousands of images of child pornography were discovered. Mr Cottis is on remand awaiting trial.*

There was a Post-it stuck to the page.

> *Thought this would interest you. Lauren Heart.*

She sat and looked at it for a long time. Then she folded it up and put it in her pocket. She cooked the evening meal, vegetable casserole as she'd said she would. It was gone six when she'd finished. Sally and Ruth were still out at work and she suddenly couldn't face being with them, answering their questions about what kind of day she had had. She didn't want to eat the vegetable casserole. She took the piece of paper out of her pocket again and tore it in half and half again and then into tiny fragments. The fact that she'd been right about Mr Cottis gave her no pleasure. She thought of Joe Bussell. She pictured him as she'd known him, a fourteen-year-old boy, physically larger than he should have been, wearing green army combats. In her mind she saw him saying goodbye to his family. *Just going out for a drink with my mates*, then taking the long slow walk from his home to Kings Cross Station. In his hand he had a carrier bag which held wire cutters and rope. *This was no spur-of-the moment decision*. His family, Lucy, his mother, the vile Stevie, none of them had known until days later.

She sat down at the table and cried.

After a while she knew she couldn't stay in. She went up to her room and put her swimsuit on under her clothes and put her beach mat and towel in a bag. It was chilly, she knew, but the sea would clear her head.

She headed for the esplanade, avoiding going anywhere near the tourist information office. The beach was almost empty; just some couples walking along and a family still digging sandcastles, the children fully dressed, perhaps having a treat after a day at school. She walked along until she found an area that was empty and laid out her beach mat. She got undressed and felt the sharp breeze nipping at her skin. The best thing was to run into the water, to get the shock of the cold over and done with quickly. She hesitated though. The sea pulsed before her, the water swinging back and forth. The surface was pitted with white and looked ragged and unwelcoming.

She carefully picked her way down the beach, the shingle digging into the soles of her feet.

She stood for a second and let a wave wash across her toes. Then she started running. She sank one clumsy foot after another into the hard wet sand, her toes catching the edges of stones, the side of her foot feeling the scratch of something thorny, and then with a dive she broke the surface of the sea and went under. For a few seconds she heard nothing; with her arms and legs tight together she propelled herself like a marine creature through the dark water and then surfaced, letting out an exclamation of shock at the cold.

She swam, one stroke after another, keeping her face down in the water, sensing the taste of salt in her mouth. When she was tired she stopped and rested. She trod water.

The beach and the esplanade looked far away.

Somewhere in the hinterland was the house she lived in with Sally and Ruth. Beyond that was the university. Beyond that was the rest of her life; the places she would go, the jobs she might have, the family she might build.

Jennifer Jones, child killer.

Would she ever be able to leave that headline behind?

She swam back and got out of the water, gingerly, taking care not to hurt her feet. She walked across the sand and picked her towel up and put it round her shoulders. Trembling with cold she sat down on the mat and stared along the beach. A couple were walking along the edge of the waves. Her eyes stayed on them as they got closer to her. In between them was a young child. They were holding his hands and every now and then they gave the child a swing in the air. The child was laughing and shouting *More, more, do it again, Dad! Mum, swing again!* The couple were young, the woman not much older than Jennifer.

They smiled at her as they passed.

Jennifer put her T-shirt on over her damp costume. Soon she would go home. It was only a ten-minute walk and she could have a hot shower and get changed.

She didn't move though. In the distance she could see the Starcross ferry making its way out of the harbour. She watched it until it disappeared.

A beeping sound came from her phone. She pulled it out of her bag. No doubt Sally was worried at seeing the vegetable casserole ready but no Jennifer anywhere around. She looked at the screen and was surprised to see the name *Jimmy Fuller*. She opened the text.

I don't care what you did in your past. I just like you now xxx

She felt a lump in her throat and held the phone for a long time, staring at the words. She sent a reply.

Thank you xxx

Moments later there came another text. She opened it.

I want to see you, tonight, now xxx

She was suddenly full of emotion. She stifled a sob.

She could meet him in a pub or she could go to his house. Why not? They could laze about on the bed, watch DVDs, or he could cook something. She could do that now because he *knew* who it was he was seeing, he was under no illusions about her. There were tears in her eyes. She wiped them away with the back of her hand and sent another text, her fingers slipping off the keys, having to backspace a couple of times to get it right.

I'd love to. Where are you?

She pulled her jeans on and shoved her sandy feet into her shoes. She could be home and changed and out again in less than thirty minutes. There was another beep. She grabbed for her phone. She opened the message.

Right behind you xx

She swung round and saw him there, on the esplanade, sitting on a bench, leaning forward, his elbows on his knees, his phone in his hand.

She rolled up her beach mat and picked up her towel. She put them both into her bag and walked towards him.

ANNE CASSIDY

Anne Cassidy lived in London for most of her life. She was a teacher for twenty years. In 1989 she started writing books for teenagers. Her first book was published in 1991 and since then she has published over forty books, thirty of which have been teen novels. She writes crime fiction and is best known for her book Looking for JJ, which was shortlisted for the Whitbread Award 2004 and the Carnegie Medal 2005. She has one son and currently lives in Essex.

www.annecassidy.com
@annecassidy6

Where the story began …

THREE CHILDREN WALKED AWAY
FROM THE EDGE OF TOWN ONE DAY
– BUT ONLY TWO OF THEM CAME BACK.

Read the original multi-award-winning

LOOKING FOR JJ

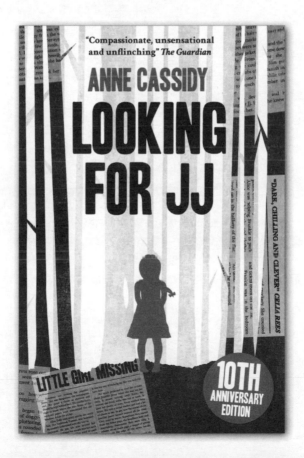